BASED ON A TRUE STORY

I0598536

ON ANOTHER SHADY MISSION

BY CHERAEE C.

Written by:

Cheraee C.

ON ANOTHER SHADY MISSION

MOCY PUBLISHING, LLC

Detroit, Michigan

ON ANOTHER SHADY MISSION

ISBN 978-1-94083-106-0
Copyright © 2014 by Cheraee C.

Published by Mocy Publishing, LLC.
Website: www.mocypublishing.com
Email: info@mocypublishing.com

All rights reserved. Except as permitted under the United States Copyright Act of 1976, no part of this publication may be reproduced or distributed in any form or by any means, or stored in a data base or retrieval system, without the prior written permission of the publisher.

Honorable Mentions to:

Mocy Publishing

Ky Hunt

Marissa Pershard

Emily Shepard

Prologue

Nobody adapts the psychology of killing overnight and for Passive the trigger she clutched that killed her ex-drug connect Champagne wasn't the first. Her past may have seemed like it was inerrant, but it wasn't. Passive had more skeletons in her closet then a haunted mansion.

The day when Passive's mug shot met the 11th precinct's booking department and Smoke was substituting for a booking officer was the historical, unthinkable day that the ultimate couple met. Smoke actually took two enthralling mug shots and fingerprints of Passive and she had the sexiest mug shot that he had ever seen. It was just everything about her that made him marvel at her unparalleled individuality.

"Passive Boone, I see you don't have any type of criminal history at all so why would you falsify your identification to a police officer?" Smoke questioned his arrestee like she was going to give him a straight answer.

"Technically I didn't falsify my identification. My nickname is Diamond so when the officer asked me for my name I said my name was Diamond. And by a glance on your badge your nickname is Smoke. I'm sure the name Smoke isn't printed anywhere on your birth certificate. I tried to explain this to the officer, but he insisted on arresting me."

"He probably just wanted to see your ass in handcuffs and be seen driving your fine ass around the city."

"If that's his idea of a fantasy then I guess."

"You must've not been staring in the mirror lately because we don't arrest women of your stature every day."

"And now your flirting. Who flirts with a woman in handcuffs? Don't I seem suspect to you? You actually believe my explanation for this disarray?" Passive asked.

"I believe you and that's exactly why I'm going to go squash this with my officers right now."

"I'm not trying to bust your little dutiful bubble, but my daddy works for the mayor so don't get your little "officer" connects misconstrued with mines. I've never made it to a holding cell before, and trust me I'm not going to see one today. Just wait on it y'all see."

Ten minutes after Passive was brought into the 11th precinct mayor Cahill's lawyer Drew was barging in the precinct's doors to free her. When the arresting officer was sitting in his squad car running Passive's information, Passive took that small window to let her daddy know what was transpiring so he could tell Cahill and Cahill could take care of it. Albeit, Passive didn't have no right to be relying on Cahill after all the unknown lunacy she was stirring up in his organization, a plug was a plug. You get what you give, and since Cahill was giving out shade, Passive was giving shade back.

Speeding was the reason the officer stopped Passive in the mist of her early bird adrenaline rush. Passive was ghostly taking down Cahill's organization and was killing off his workers one by one, and had just successfully killed another disloyal employee which would make it her fifth slaying.

Mayor Cahill was supposed to be an honorable man and Passive's godfather, but what kind of godfather propositions his goddaughter for sex? What kind of godfather hires one of his workers to try to take his goddaughter's virginity? What kind of godfather is the number one suspect in your goddaughter's mother's unfortunate disappearance?

Of course Passive's father Syrian knew nothing about all these things that were manifesting behind his daughter's closed curtains. If he would've found out Cahill would've been ten feet under. Passive couldn't bear to be the reason why her father spent the rest of his life in the prison system so she kept his shadiness on the hush and found a silent way to deal with her definition of redemption. Since her daddy was a professional security guard, a gun instructor, a nightclub security manager to over five nightclub establishments in the D, a single father, plus plenty more job fortes, Syrian had to instill his security skills within his daughter.

Smoke was the only man that Passive had ever shared all of her innermost secrets with and that's exactly how they made it to become a ride or die couple. The day that finally shined light on the true Cahill was Passive's father's murder. She had always been contemplating the day that they would cross paths again. She knew it was going to be soon, she just didn't know when. All Passive knew was her crazy life created a street girl named Diamond who was not to be underestimated, underrated, or understated.

Table of Contents

Chapter 1:

100 miles to Payback

3 months after Smoke's disappearance

Cool, tenacious gusts of midnight air were lingering up, down, under, and around Passive's pores, but nothing was cold to her anymore except for love. It was cold that her one true love was stripped away from her by Lindsay (the wicked witch of the west coast.) In Passive's sharp and torn eyes the only person that had the holy power to strip anybody away from anybody is God, and since Lindsay sure as hell wasn't God, wasn't godly, didn't know any gods, and probably would never even meet God, she had best to watch her rearview mirrors closely because Passive was coming for her and there wasn't no way around that.

Fog lights were beaming, motorcycles of all makes and models were parked in precision, and masses of motorcycle club members and associates were gathered in crowds and circles waiting on the Saturday night races to roar and rumble. Everything was going down on Grand River and W. Grand Boulevard behind the Tabernacle

Temple. The first race of the night was going to be the best race that had ever taken place in motorcycle racing history.

"So what's your bet apple pie?" The Sergeant-of-Arms for *The Monarchs* asked Passive.

"Cruise now you know that's not how it works. You ain't even go holler at Gab yet about his bet. You run right along while I talk to Diamond right quick, and don't say shit in rebuttal cuz everybody around here knows I don't play word games."

"Elvia glad you stopped by, I was just having a little fun with the newest rider to our competition, but since you in a vibe killing mood I'll go talk to Gab."

Soon as Cruise darted off Diamond prepared to check this meddlesome stranger. Ain't no telling why the spokesman was shook by her, and whatever the case was who gives a damn because tonight was all about Diamond and Gab, the big race, the big payback.

"I don't know you from a can of paint and you don't know me either so why are you interrupting my flow?"

"I'm just trying to warn you because these niggas around here will swish you around and then spit your little perky ass out. I've seen the darkest days of too many girls like you who try to win a game that they know nothing about and got too much pride to listen."

"Well Elvia you listen now and you listen good; I know all about this game, and I do everything I do for a reason. I'm not here by coincidence or for a stupid, puny street title, and I damn sure didn't just start racing, riding, or gambling yesterday. I'm pretty sure it's some needy bitches around here that need some guidance so why don't you go find them and potty train them with your wisdom, but this chick right here Diamond is good and like you I don't need no rebuttal because I don't play word games either." Diamond's tongue was sharp as hell, but she didn't

15

care who she offended. Whoever this Elvia chick was, she needed to stay in her lane and just "watch" like everybody else. Diamond was going to show you better then she could tell you.

Quickly, Diamond got herself back in the racing mind frame. She knew this was a dirty game, and she came prepared with strategies to make sure Gab didn't make it to the finish line if he even saw the finish line in front of him after she was done with him. Cruise was back on the scene.

"You so pretty Diamond if Gab wins can I give you a kiss like the Princess and the Frog?"

"Cut the shit, and get to it Cruise."

"Okay Gab says if he wins he wants 5 racks and he wants a threesome with you and Elvia when the race is over."

"Is that his bitch or something because one man can't even handle me, so what do he need two bitches for?"

"She just one of the finest bitches around here he haven't smashed next to you."

"Bet and if I win I want 10 racks, I want his bike, his colors, and I want him to complete his next race naked."

"That's a hell of a bet!" The high and drunken mass shouted.

Pause:

All of this may seem new, but nothing is new with Passive/Diamond. Smoke used to love riding his motorcycle into the sunset, so much so that he taught Passive how to ride. It was a long journey, but Passive refused to give up until she mastered it just as well as him. Before Smoke became an official cop, Gab asked Smoke if he could race with his bike. Once Smoke married Passive she became his pride and joy so he didn't mind letting his cousin Gab use his bike because he trusted him. And trust is where people always fail because Gab bet a race on Smoke's bike and lost. Gab didn't even have enough balls to tell Smoke that he lost his bike racing. He made a bitch ass excuse saying somebody stole Smoke's bike outside this female house he was chilling with that night. Eventually Gab won the bike back, but he never returned it to Smoke. Gab kept it like it was his, since Smoke cut his ties with Gab and most of his family members. What's mines is mines whether we beefing or not, you never take somebody else's possessions and claim them as yours especially not family. Even though, Smoke and Gab weren't cool like that no more, Gab could've dropped the bike off, and left it parked in the driveway or something anonymous, but I guess dumb minds don't think like that. But tonight Diamond was going to get Smoke's bike back, and make sure Gab paid for all of his foolishness. As a woman, you never forget anything that a man teaches you especially when he teaches you something useful.

Play:

Gab had no idea that he was about to be racing his cousin's wife Passive because he was dealing with Diamond, the name Diamond was all he knew. All his homies were gloating about Diamond's volcanic beauty and her amiable bike, and if his homies were gloating about this chick and nobody had ever seen or smashed her before he wanted first dibs. He wanted to see what all the hype was about, and get another successful race up under his undefeated leather belt, so he headed for the flags and the marks. Diamond already had her helmet on and was waiting for Gab on her bike.

"Are you done playing with yourself? Can we get this race going?" The crowd went wild while Gab was eye-fucking the fabrics off of Diamond. Gab had fucked so many girls that he couldn't even sense any familiarity with Diamond.

"Nothing will compare to the nut I'm going to bust when I win this race." Gab had one of his groupies put on his helmet as he sat on his bike and put his bike in place.

3-2-1- let's go!

"Ladies first!"

Gab let Diamond get a head start when in reality he was the one who needed the head start. Diamond scurried off like a car does in a high speed police chase. Stuck on crowd antics, Gab took off in the air with a back willy until he was riding side by side with Diamond. Once he was gaining on Diamond he took off in the air again in front willy mode, Diamond tossed a gang of steel tacks on the raceway causing Gab's bike to get side-tracked, him to shoot off of it like a geyser in the sky while his bike just stopped itself and sat frozen. Diamond was long gone, past the finish line, and victory was hers.

Riding back to Gab, Passive stuck her hand out for her 10 bands which Gab slapped it in her hand. Gab's internal feelings was priceless, just as much as his exterior nonsense was trying to front like everything was cool when he really wanted to re-race Diamond and double-up his money. Now that he was temporarily handicapped, Gab wasn't about to be re-racing shit not even a neighborhood rat. He was mortified, he was ashamed, and he was the laughing stock of the night.

"I don't care how you hand it to me just put it in my head." Of course Gab damn sure didn't want to come off no 10 bands, but a bet is a bet. Next time Gab will think twice about gambling with strangers.

Diamond didn't care to say anything else to him because a bet was a bet, and since she had a shit load of witnesses to prove he lost, and he was injured, no other words between them needed to be spoken because it could be months or years before his ass ever rode a motorcycle again.

Unfortunately when Gab shot off his bike it caused him to suffer a fractured femur and he ended up being transported to Henry Ford Hospital on W. Grand Boulevard. Elvia showed herself once again after Passive won the race.

"I guess I underestimated you," Elvia added.

"You did, but everybody does until they get to know me."

"So how are you going to get the bike home? It's only one of you."

"Well since your so concerned about it, why don't you ride it to my house and I'll give you a ride back to the city or wherever it is you reside."

Exactly as planned Elvia followed Passive to her place until they ended in Passive's spacious driveway.

"I'll be right back I'm going to go in the house to get my car keys so I can drop you off."

Elvia just nodded her head in agreement, but when Passive came back outside and leered around Elvia had vanished.

She's outré, but I really didn't want to give the chick a ride anyway. Its bad enough she knows where I live now. Hopefully by it still being pitch black outside and all the loops, twists, and sharp turns we took she'll forget. I wonder who else I would have asked if she hadn't volunteered. I usually never need back up. The only back-up I ever needed was from Smoke. It doesn't matter though because everything worked itself out anyway.

So Passive locked the bikes and the house up and called it a night.

$

Everybody loved the name Passive so much that people's sensation of food was jealous of their sensation of words. Cruise rode to the hospital in the ambulance truck with Gab whose real name was Cajon Carter since that was his best friend. Instead of concentrating on his injury, he couldn't stop yapping about his last defeat. It was too mind-boggling to be real, and even though he was in agonizing pain, he was more concerned about winning and setting his record straight. In no way, shape, form, or fashion was a woman going to get away with taking his undefeated title.

"I still can't believe a woman just ganked me out of 10 stacks, my bike, and all that other dumb shit she said. She rode that bike too fucking good like my cousin Smoke. And why would a girl won't to be compensated with a motorcycle unless it had some sentimental value to her or something? Why would a girl want to humiliate me like that in front of my whole squad and put my ass up in the hospital?"

"Well trick no motherfucking good bro."

"Now that I think about it, that girl I was racing was my cousin's wife Passive; it had to be."

"Did they give you some kind of drugs or something because I could've sworn that girl told me her name was Diamond?"

"That must be her cover-up name or something, but if that chick got green eyes it's her. I swear it's her."

"If that is your cousin's wife tell him I said I'm Mr. Steal Your Girl, and I will take his bitch and make her roll them green eyes back and forth like Aaliyah said."

"Negro please, you couldn't get Passive even if you won the Mega Million. You might be foaming in the mouth over her, but me, I cannot and I will not let this shit ride. Ain't no bitch never fucked over Gab before, and ain't no bitch going to fuck over Gab now."

"Aye don't call my future wife a bitch son. And why you in the red zone your name is Cajon. Ain't nobody about to be calling you Gab in here."

"I swear sometimes I don't know what planet you came from but, you just called her a bitch doe so why is it a problem when I call her a bitch?"

"She whopped your ass fair and square, why can't you take your ass whooping like a man?"

"That bitch cheated; she had to do some type of slick pulla ass shit. That's why my ass laying up in an ambulance on a gurney not because I personally fucked up some shit. She did this to me."

"What did you do to her because women don't try to kill you unless they got ammunition to?"

"It's some old ancient shit that doesn't have anything to do with her."

"I guess she representing then like Kelly Rowland say. If her man got beef with you she got beef with you too."

"So now we got beef with them then."

Since beef was declared and Gab made it safe and sound to the hospital, and the doctors were getting him together, Gab left him in one peace to get some shuteye and to go conjure up something real shady with their boys. Sorry Diamond/Passive whoever you are, but you messed with the wrong captain at the wrong motorcycle club, and now you're going to wish that you would've left all well alone.

Chapter 2:

Irrelevancy Never Fades

Exes can never accept the fact that they are exes...

Passive's pillow was her two hands cupped to the side of her face, while her head rested on her hands and on the arm of her and Smoke's favorite leather loveseat. And her blanket was the spirit of Smoke's body heat transmitting through her chilly wonders. As much as Passive hated sleeping alone, she hated sleeping in her and Smoke's bedroom alone too so she avoided her bedroom by any means until her king's return.

Now an easy-sleeper, Passive was awoken by the slightest peeps, squeaks, or squeals, and out of nowhere she heard her phone ascending.

"This Diamond."

"Diamond, I keep hearing a lot of cats with Smoke's name in their mouths like he home or something. What's really good with that? Is Smoke home for real? Are y'all living in conspiracy because that shit would be out cold?"

"Spare your fucking rumors for his paparazzi. Diamond only listens to facts, details, physical descriptions, and so forth. Unless you got the rundown on that hang up, rethink, and try that shit again."

Either idiotism is a dominant gene, or my generation is just full of a bunch of fucking idiots and dingbats. I can't never catch a break or get a cat nap in without somebody raising my blood pressure.

The remedial phone call she just received was her Q to get up and get to the black bottom of why Smoke's name was floating around the city like a sheet of an old sales paper. Diamond detested following street leads, but she would either live to regret, live to explore, and/or live to punish. Smoke didn't marry no fool. Diamond knew damn well the ears on your head weren't the only pair of ears she needed to conquer the world as they saw it. She needed ears everywhere, ears on the corners, ears in the 11th precinct, ears in the cities they reign, ears, ears, ears. And that's exactly why people say be careful what you say because you never know whose listening.

After some quick bathe flow, a quick cocoa butter rub down, and a little biker chick outfit, Diamond grabbed her a Naked Strawberry Banana smoothie out the fridge and kept it pushing to the streets so when one of her many loyal informants called back, she would already be in the centerfold of all the action.

Parked in a secure alley between some tall, rickety structures and green, grass covered parking lots, Diamond was pre-mediating her next move.

Finally, Diamond got another call.

"I hope you got all of your bases covered this time," Diamond warned the person on the other end of the phone because if they didn't she was liable to go find that bitch and bang that bitch head into the pavement.

"Solei Mack is the name that you need to know. Solei is actually one of Smoke's ex-girlfriends from back in the day. She is a tall, petite, chocolate fee, who lives downtown in the Woodbridge Estates who's been telling everybody that she is housing Smoke so she can get the 10,000 reward money for finding him. She been Instagramming everybody in the streets a photo shopped picture of her and Smoke together like they is really one happy couple. Everybody knows that bitch lying because she don't know shit about you, the picture looks to fucking fake, she don't know shit about Smoke being married, or Lindsay Chambers, I mean."

"What the fuck did you just say?"

The caller hung up instantaneously realizing that the conversation was getting a little bit too casual and she may have overstepped her word boundaries.

Just as Diamond was about to redial a bitch, she realized the caller had called private, but her husband wasn't a cop for no reason. She was about to use her tablet to trace the caller's number, just like Smoke taught her. Thirty seconds went by and she had a number just like that.

Now Diamond was playing the private caller game with one of her throwaway phones.

"How in the fuck do you know Lindsay Chambers?" Diamond demanded after she got an alert greeting. The lady on the other end had been stalling for weeks, but she was ready to expose herself.

"I've been feeding you leads for weeks. What you think I've been doing this shit for fun or something?"

"Fuck you and your leads, tell me how the fuck do you know Lindsay Chambers before I be sitting inside your living room in 2.2 seconds?"

"I know Lindsay Chambers because she is my enemy just as live as she is yours. I use to work for her until a deal went bad and she tried to have me killed. Now the shoe is on the other foot except I don't need to hire anybody to do my dirty work."

"Basically you got a hit on your head, and I got a hit on my head so we should be best fucking friends? No, your problems are exactly your problems so you handle that shit and keep me and my husband out of your itinerary. Thank you for your leads, but I'll pass on your services."

This is exactly why I don't deal with bitches because they too fucking needy. I need you, you need me, everybody needs somebody; incorrect bitches I don't need nobody except my husband Smoke. And I don't need nothing except for y'all bored bitches to stop tryna get some limelight.

Passive hurried up and ended this senseless call with an operator.

$

It was time for Diamond to ride out on this bitch Solei running around town with the loose lips. *Since that bitch like talking and falsifying pictures this bitch goin be in the red light district tonight.*

Diamond got Solei's permanent address just as quick as she retrieved her caller's phone number. Already programmed in her GPS navigation she took off burning, tire screeching, rubber.

Chapter 3:

I Spy Elvia Parrish

I was born to pop off…….

Derived from Dade County, Florida Elvia was a survivor. She didn't have any brothers or sisters, or a mother or father to rescue her from the tangled streets. At 11, the year of puberty, Elvia's mother and father were sold to some Columbian sex-traffickers because they chose to gamble their lives to Ramon noodle specks. Together, her mother and father had accumulated a 100,000 gambling debt in a month's time with no kind of input. Thank goodness the Columbians didn't know that Elvia's parents had a daughter because then Elvia would've been sold into the impious world of drugs and sex also.

After her parents were smuggled away by their new owners, Elvia then put her faith into her neighbor Posh. Posh didn't know anything about kids, because she didn't have any kids, and she would never be an aunt because she too was sibling-less. Posh promised Elvia's parents if anything happened to them that she would be Elvia's guardian, and now it was time for her to gratify her promise.

Posh was 24 and she was an up and coming female MC. Posh was 5'5' with brown eyes, had a smile like the sunrise, and a body like a Victoria Secret model. Glued to a game dominated by men, Posh was determined to make a name for herself so she was always doing showcases, shows, mix-tapes, and in the studio, and like Posh's little sister, Elvia was always attached like adhesive to Posh's hips until one studio day when Elvia was 12. Elvia broke loose to use the bathroom while Posh was dropping 16 bars on a song.

A simple bathroom break turned out to be the worst day of Elvia's life. When Elvia was in route to the ladies room, a rapper by the name of J-Bow was trailing behind her. Once Elvia was secured in a stall, squatted, peed, and was in the process of pulling her denim jeans up, J-Bow bust in.

"What are you doing J-Bow? Leave me alone!"

"I got a gift for you, ain't no point in screaming ain't nobody going to hear you anyway."

J-Bow started pulling his pants down and positioning Elvia to take her virginity.

"Posh! Posh! Posh!" Elvia yelled countless times until her throat was dry and sore.

"I paid Posh five stacks for this very moment with you so just get with the program."

Unsure of what was going on and who was playing her, Elvia got tired of fighting, and started crying in piercing pain. She remembered that Posh gave her a knife she kept in her sock in case anybody ever bothered her. Blood had already been gushing down, and the aches of rape were becoming too real.

Since J-Bow wanted to play with little girls not knowing what they were capable of, Elvia figured she'll play some games of her own.

"Can I put it in my mouth J-Bow?" J-Bow couldn't believe his ears.

"Hell yeah you can." Elvia turned around facing J-Bow and bent down and licked the head of his penis as she reached down in her sock for that silver sharp thing that was about to change everything.

She got it in her grip, pushed the clasps to open it and struck him right in his penis.

"Stupid little foul bitch!" J-Bow yelled pulling himself out of the stall and turning around to look in the mirror. Right after Elvia stabbed him in his nuts, Posh came, soon as she didn't see Elvia through the booth.

"Elvia!" Posh yelled through the studio's halls.

"I'm in the bathroom Posh help me!"

Entering the security code for the restroom (9-1-2-4), Posh came late, but late was better than never. Seeing the demoralizing scene that was before her she was instantly angered. It was the blood, the sex, the aroma in

40

the air, the crummy look on J-Bow's face, and the broken look on Elvia's face. Elvia was Posh's heart, and nobody would ever, ever violate her again on Posh's time.

"Elvia go in the stall now and close your ears okay!"

Elvia pulled the gun out of the clip on her left ankle.

"So you like raping little girls and out of all the little girls you could've raped you goin rape my fam J-Bow! Is that how we roll now J-Bow?"

"Be proud of yourself she stuck me real good in the nuts. She cutthroat just like you I see."

"You damn right, but I promise you will never rape another little girl after today," Posh exclaimed then pulled her trigger and let off two shots. One shot to the left temple, and another shot to the right temple."

"Now fanaticize that."

"Come on Elvia we got to go." Immediately Posh grabbed Elvia and kept her from looking at J-Bow's dead

41

body, but Elvia knew Posh had killed him. After that incident, Posh quit rapping and her and Elvia laid low for awhile until Posh sold her house. Once Posh sold her house, they moved up north to a quiet suburb in Canton, Michigan so her and Elvia could get a fresh start. Now that Elvia was getting a little older it was definitely time for Posh to educate Elvia's uneducated mind. Face it, Elvia was 13, had already stabbed somebody, been raped, witnessed a murder, didn't have no type of education, or no type of stability in her life. All Posh knew how to do was kill and now she was about to school Elvia, but only if Elvia wanted to embark on that path. Unlike most parents or guardians, Posh refused to force a profession on Elvia. Everything that she was doing was exactly because it was what Elvia wanted to do.

Posh was a paid hit woman for the biggest heroin drug distributor in the U.S.A (Blanco). Posh was paid for contract killing, cold blooded assassinations, torture, and even pre-meditated natural deaths. The day Blanco got killed and replaced was the day before Elvia's parents were bartered into sex slavery. Posh could've worked for the replacement, but her loyalty was declared to Blanco and plus she was tired of being an on call killer anyway. She had lots of money put up from her late night slayings so Elvia and her were A1 like A1 steak sauce, but there was always the what if's. What if something happened to Posh then what? Then Posh was going to leave Elvia with all her money, and everything she owned, and at least she would make sure Elvia was well-prepared to fend for herself.

Elvia was a fast-learner and at 16, she had everything programmed in her memory bank and memorized. She knew the makes and models of any type of gun whether it was legal or illegal. She knew how to use a gun, she had perfect aim, and she knew karate. She knew exactly how to utilize technology for her criminal mind, and how to cover her tracks. She knew how to drive a car, a van, a SUV, a motorcycle, a commercial truck; anything with 2 or more wheels leading her up to having an enhanced license with a passport because hittas take many forms. She knew all about the female and male anatomy and quick ways to stop blood flow. She knew how to conceal her weapons, and of course Posh had to teach Elvia about her body, sex, pleasure, and how to use it to her advantage.

When Elvia turned 18, Posh was ready to let Elvia spread her wings.

"I've taken care of you and watched over you for a long time, and no matter what I will always be here for you, but now that your grown, I'm ready to go on some adventures of my own," Posh explained, "but I promise to keep tabs on you for the rest of your life."

"I don't want you to go Posh, but I know you have to."

"I got you covered Elvia open your hand." Posh placed a band of 20 g's in Elvia's possession knowing damn well that would hold her over until she got herself established and found her somebody to run hits for.

"I'm really going to miss you Posh and I want to thank you for everything that you've done for me," so Elvia and Posh hugged goodbye and now Elvia was completely solo like a lead singer is after he/she branches off from a musical group.

Eventually, Elvia found her a little shot girl gig at the Flight Club in Inkster which is one of the most exalted gentlemen's clubs in Michigan. Amenities included over 10,000 square feet, crystal rooms, VIP Martini Bar, and daily specials which coincidentally caused her to meet Lindsay Chambers. Lindsay was looking for a female hitta to work in her organization she claimed to be a drug cartel at the time. Eventually, years after working for Lindsay and after making millions of bands with Lindsay, she learned that Lindsay Chambers wasn't the woman she claimed to be. She realized Lindsay was a shady bitch who just owned a magazine and hired people like Elvia to kill people who were in the way of her happiness or her joy. The moment of clarity for this revelation, was when Elvia met Omani. Meager Omani was always on the edge until Omani opened up to Elvia about how she felt awful for working for Lindsay under her conditions. Omani revealed to Elvia that she was Lindsay's ex-boyfriend sister and that Lindsay was trying to get Omani to help her break up her brother's marriage to his wife Passive. Omani got real deep with Elvia so deep that she shared the standpoints of her acidic relationships with her brother, her sister Kyra, and Passive. Plenty of times when Elvia and Lindsay were schmoozing in the office, Elvia always noticed shady leads against this alleged Passive Mitchell. When Lindsay put Omani and Passive on the front cover of her magazine, she knew that shit was unreal and self-made. Like hell, Lindsay got

Passive and Omani together, in one room, in her studio in front of one of her photographers to shoot cover shots. Enough was enough, so Elvia went to Lindsay herself after her last hit and quit. As Elvia was on the way to her house, she realized that she was being followed. Come to find out Lindsay had contracted a killer Reno to kill her dead, but Elvia was taught by America's finest so she flipped the script on Reno and killed him first with a bullet to the head in her backyard. Outside was the best side, because Elvia wasn't about to get no blood on her perfectly unstained carpet.

From that day forward Elvia and Lindsay were enemies and Lindsay didn't even know it. Funny, most of the people that Lindsay set out to kill were never killed if they were even touched or grazed by a bullet. And just like Lindsay, Elvia began to feel some type of way about Passive Mitchell because she knew more about Passive Mitchell now then her own husband probably did.

Chapter 4:

Dual Energy

Can you liberate me?

In her 2nd trimester of pregnancy, Omani was so emotional which was a popular pregnant side effect. It was all those emotions she had outside of pregnancy that was getting in the way of her embracing motherhood. Nowadays Smoke was going to be Uncle Smoke and Passive was going to be Aunt Passive, and Kyra was going to be Aunt Kyra, but who knew when or if any of them was going to have shit to do with her ever again. Sometimes new babies, nephews, or nieces didn't change shit and as Omani felt it, she was responsible for Passive's kidnapping and she was responsible for Smoke's kidnapping. She knew from day one that Lindsay Chambers was plotting against the both of them and never squealed a peep. Omani tried and tried repetitively to reach out to Passive, but Passive didn't entertain shit from Omani's mouth, only shit that was pertaining to the baby.

As for Omani and Onyx's relationship, it was now back in the on again and off again stages. Since Onyx's supposed one night stand Tia was pregnant also, it was like Omani was sharing Onyx with Tia. Onyx had to be there for Omani, Onyx had to be there for Tia, it was a constant tug of war and somebody had to end up in the mud. That somebody just had to be Omani. How could she blame Onyx though for wanting some outer space from her? They were nearly homeless because of Omani, they had to keep a low profile because of Omani, they were supposed to be dead and gone because of Omani, everything was Omani's fault except for the baby that is. Omani didn't ask to be pregnant, Onyx chose that decision, but clearly he chose that decision with somebody else also.

Omani's heart was in knots because Tia was just supposed to be a red herring. Who bangs red herrings raw and then impregnates them? She was definitely beneath side bitch status, but that was only based upon the bullshit Onyx had filled her head with. It really wasn't no telling how long Onyx had truly been messing with Tia or even if the baby she was carrying was really his. At the moment Omani had a thought and she wasn't going to give up until her thought was fulfilled. She planned on planting a bunch of bugs in Onyx's head just like he was doing her to make Tia take a prenatal DNA paternity test ASAP. Omani always said," why wait for tomorrow, when you don't know if you're going to make it today".

$

Little did Omani know, Tia was not the ploy, Omani was the ploy.

"Little Onyx is getting hungry," Tia complained as she caressed her stomach and rested her head on Onyx like he was a headrest.

"Oh is he, I'm getting hungry too, "Onyx massaged Tia's stomach back.

"Real talk babe, I think we need to go get a ring guard or something because I almost lost my ring today when I was messing around in the baby's room."

"Doctor's orders say you supposed to be on bed rest. I don't need you to be doing anything to risk my son. You tell me what you want done and I'll do it. I'll take your ring to the jeweler tomorrow, and I'm going to get in his ass for not sizing it correctly."

"Everything is still so surreal to me, but it's amazing how life has worked itself out after all the Omani shit."

"Bay we having a good day please don't mention her name. I told you to stop mentioning her name around my son anyway. He can hear you. Besides you won, you got the ring, and I'm here with you. Why can't we just be happy?"

"We can be happy now especially since you made her get an abortion, and you officially moved out. Now your only tied to me and your son."

Every since Onyx knocked up both Omani and Tia he's been having a joy ride with the both of them. Onyx has been telling Tia that Omani got an abortion and terminated

her pregnancy, and she kicked him out their new apartment.

And Onyx has taken it even further to propose to Tia. Onyx

has been telling Omani that Tia is on bed-rest and that he

goes over her house occasionally as her caretaker. He's also

been telling her that he's been staying at his best friend

Rue's house since him and Omani weren't on good terms.

Onyx was full of lies, lies, and more lies, and Onyx's lies

were bound to come back and bite him in the ass sooner

then he estimated.

$

Diamond had been waiting on nightfall all day so

she could strike. Her clips were loaded and her side

weapons were intact too. Good thing Solei stayed on the

end condo on W. Contour. Just as Diamond was getting

ready to depart her vehicle, a knock came to her window so

Diamond laid one of her pistols on her lap and rolled her

window down slightly. When Diamond made eye contact

with the stranger on the other side of her window, she realized it was that Elvia chick again who stuck her gun inside Passive's window.

"Let me in I need to talk to you right away."

"It seems like you always want to talk right before the action happens." Not wanting to start a gun war in the middle of the Woodbridge's and wanting to finish what she came to do, she decided to hear Elvia out.

"Do you have a tracking device on my car or something?"

"No I just know how you think and I know how to find you."

"Why are you here I don't need no babysitter?"

"I know all about you Passive Mitchell so cut the shit." *This bitch knows my government name maybe I should soften up a bit.* "I've played your shadow for far too long. Now it's time to get real. I know your sister-in-law

Omani, I know Lindsay Chambers, I know your past, I know your present, and I probably even know your future."

"So Lindsay sent you here?"

"I'm here because you and I come from the same muscle. Lindsay crossed me and now I'm crossing her by teaming up with the woman she has been after for years. I want to kill her and you want to kill her. She's expecting you to kill her though, but she's not expecting me to kill her because she thinks I'm dead. You might think you know it all, but you really don't, and everything you don't know I know."

"How do I know you're not just telling me all of this to trap me?"

"Lindsay is somewhere in no man's land with your husband trying to brainwash him and do all types of indescribable things to him. Do you honestly think she has time to hire people to come after you? That bitch knows she hot as hell right now and if she makes one wrong move everything will fall out of place. She's not going to risk getting caught especially as much time and money it has taken her to get to where's she at. Undoubtedly, you don't know Lindsay like I do. It was her envy for you that made me quit working for her. You sell drugs and I kill people for a living. You just started killing people, but I was subjected into this lifestyle. Your only killing in revenge, but if it wasn't for that your hands would be sparkling clean because you left the killing up to Smoke, but now you can leave the killing up to me."

"I've changed a lot since Smoke has been gone and yes I have become very callous. Your right about a lot of things, but I'm the one who's being violated here by these people so fine I'll let you help me, but once we kill Lindsay you can vanish into thin air just like you did the other night."

"Deal and there's one more thing?"

"You think you're walking into a condo with just Solae, but she has a roommate and her name is Kali."

"So you kill Kali and I'll kill Solei let's go."

Hopping out of Passive's black GMC Terrain SUV, Elvia picked the condo lock's, closed the door soundlessly behind them, and entered the condo. Standing on the Welcome placemat, all Elvia and Diamond heard was outrageous moaning and squealing bed springs from upstairs. *She said they was roommates not fuck buddies, but I guess that's what the new term of roommate's is.* Elvia signaled for them to go up the stairs so they went foot by foot, and eased their selves to the top floor in a follow the leader motion.

Elvia went in for the execution. She hit the lights on those two scrawny naked bitches with Diamond covering her. Solei and Kali were facing her headboard as she was hammering Kali's woo-ha from the back. Right away, both of them stopped and rearranged themselves to face the strangers in their house.

"The fucking is over now I need both of y'all to hit the floor and get on all fours right now!"

"My door was locked how did y'all get in?" Solei asked bamboozled why somebody would want to kill her.

"So what does that mean? Locks are meant to be broken." Elvia answered.

If staring was a contest, the chick Kali would've won because she couldn't keep her eyes off of Passive.

"Oh my god it's you, Passive. I never thought I would ever see your fine ass in person, but since I am really seeing you this is exactly how I would imagine it. I don't know what you and your little sidekick got going on, but I know how you get down. I think you came here to play not to kill." Passive was beyond offended.

I've never seen this twisted bitch a day in my life. How in the fuck does she know my name and what the fuck does she mean she know how I get down? She the one getting fucked the shit out of by a girl, but she got the audacity to tell me she knows how I get down. I swear the nerve of bitches talking they miscellaneous bullshit. If she knew me, she would know that I don't play with bitches. If I come for you, then it's definitely to kill you.

In response to Kali's comment Diamond thudded her pistol across Kali's wet mouth. "Why do you think my name is Passive and what do you mean you know how Passive gets down because personally I don't think your bird brain ass knows shit?"

Without any hesitations Kali inched her left hand at the edge of Solei's mattress, slightly lifted it up, and grabbed the knife that was planted between the mattress and the box spring. Before Elvia or Diamond could shoot her up, Kali sliced her own throat like she had been anticipating slicing her throat for years.

This was supposed to be two murders, not one suicide and one murder, but whatever the case was going to be, Diamond and Elvia had a new set of punches to roll with.

"So before you kill yourself too like your home girl did where the fuck is Smoke Solei?" Diamond asked striking Solei in the face with her pistol knocking her off balance.

"I'm not telling you where he's at until I get my money, and since y'all ain't cops I plead the fifth."

Diamond smacked her again and all of a suddenly Diamond lowered herself to the floor when she realized Solei didn't have a strap-on on. Solei was a he/she. She had a penis dangling from her crouch and a pussy.

"What the fuck are you a hermaphrodite?"

"Smoke liked it," Solei stuck her tongue out and flicked it at Diamond.

"Say Smoke name one more time and I promise you I will cut your little wee-wee off and your tongue at the same damn time before you kill yourself! I'm sure he thought you were a normal chick until he got your ass naked."

"What are you fucking him or something why are you so defensive?" Elvia kicked Solei in her nuts like she was a nigga.

"This bitch not going to talk either so just let her ice herself and let's keep it moving," Elvia instructed Diamond.

"Oh I get it he's not your man you like girls too just like me right? Why would you want to kill somebody who is just like you?"

"Bitch boom, ain't shit about you and I alike."

Elvia used her foot to slide the bloody knife over to Solei's reach.

"Kill yourself you old abnormal bitch," Elvia ordered.

Trying to decide exactly how she wanted to die, Solei figured she mine as well kill herself because it was no way in hell she was going to make it out of her house alive or these two crazy bitches standing before her were going to let her live so she took the knife and sliced her throat just like her friend did.

And just like that, the job was done. Only issue was the girl that killed herself was not Solei's roommate Kali; it was just another one of Solei's floozies that she had been banging for months and her name was Novara Chambers. Novara was kin to the Chamber's family that included Lindsay Chambers which made Novara one of Lindsay's young, hot cousins. Novara knew who Passive really was from when she was on Lindsay's magazine cover kissing Omani which was the girl on girl action Novara was referring too. And even though Novara wasn't the girl that

Diamond set out to kill knowing that she eliminated one

less Chamber family member would be a liberation to her,

but long as Solei was deceased that was all that mattered.

Chapter 5

Tit for Tat

Fair exchange no robbery....

Age and health was kin to each other. Both factors dismembered lives, families, and bodies like serial killers. Unfortunately, for Liz Chambers, her health and her age had her drafting up her homemade will.

After overstaying her welcome for 2 and ½ decades at the Rose Hill Center, Liz's services were indefinitely terminated there. The gates of hell were calling Liz, so the Rose Hill Center abnegated her to die at home.

Since Lindsay was in the corporate business of stealing loved ones, Passive was in the hollow-tip business of killing loved ones one by one until finally she got to Lindsay Chambers whether Smoke and Passive reunited or not. Passive was ready to attack Lindsay's family tree and the person at the peak of the tree was Lindsay's mother-Liz Chambers. Spouses and children were usually the most commonly used live bait for criminal affairs, but in Lindsay's case she didn't have a spouse and she didn't have any kids, so next in line was her parents. Being that she was a female, Passive was sure she would get more of a rise out of Lindsay if she killed Lindsay's mother instead of Lindsay's father.

Passive was digging up dirt on Liz Chambers like she was a federal prosecutor. She was set aback when she found out that Mrs. Chambers spent most of her life in a nut-house and was diagnosed with mental illness. And she was even more set aback when she found out that Lindsay was born in the same nut-house her mother was harbored in, and that Lindsay too was diagnosed with mental illness and spent a couple years upstate in the snake-pit too.

No wonder that bitch is so delusional, she was born mentally ill. I wonder if Smoke knew anything about her mental history because if he did he should've told me. I bet that bitch thought she had a secret, but no secret goes without exposure.

Uncertain about how Passive was going to kill Liz at a mental institute, Passive was relieved when Elvia told her that Liz was released from the cookoo asylum that held the oxygen to her era. Now that Liz was right up under Passive's nose, Passive was just waiting for that killer instinct to kick in and say *it's time to kill that bitch.*

Elvia was going to kill Corset and Passive was going to kill Liz. That was the plan and they were sticking to it. Every night the lights went out at ten pm sharp and it got dark around eight-ish so nine o'clock was the time. Passive put her shady countenance on and rung Liz's doorbell like she was an UPS deliverer.

"Welcome to the Chamber's residence where everybody is a slave, how can I help you two dolls?" A black woman with a maid outfit on answered who Passive knew was the help Corset.

"We are good friends of Lindsay's and she sent these red roses and balloons to give to her mother."

"That is so darling of her. Her mother has been very upset that Lindsay hasn't contacted her yet or came to see her. I'm sure this will shut her up though. Please come in."

"We apologize for coming so late, but our flights were delayed."

"I remember back in the day when I use to travel the world. Needless to say a dying bitch, I mean woman needs visitors."

"Word," Elvia agreed.

"I really have to tinkle can I please use your ladies room madam?" Elvia gallantly asked Corset.

"Please call me Corset. I'm going to show girly to Mrs. Chamber's dungeon and then I'll show you where the main toilet system is."

"By all means I'll just wait right here."

Before Passive knew it she was scrolling through Mrs. Chambers chambers'.

"Corset you brought me a guest. Who is this little pretty bitch?" *Who is this old bag calling a bitch? She called me a pretty bitch, but still she called me a bitch like she been knowing me since elementary or something.*

"She's good friends with Lindsay. Your daughter finally sent you some gifts. Please don't scare her away. You don't get visitors very often."

"Oh okay leave us Corset," Mrs. Chambers demanded after Corset fluffed her pillows and tucked her comforter.

"So what is your name girl?"

"My name is Passive."

"Who in the hell named you that girl an emotion? Your mother must be named Faith or something oblivious like that huh?"

Passive didn't find shit funny about her name or Liz trying to throw shade to her mother, but she took it as humor.

"Humor is the last sense I got left honey so don't be offended. What has my crooked daughter been doing these days?"

"She's been kidnapping people's husbands. Do you by any chance remember her ex-boyfriend Smoke?"

"Yeah I do."

"Well that's my husband and your daughter kidnapped him. Now you got to pay for her mistakes. Think of my heart as a pie that's split into four slices because that's the way my heart feels and there are four chambers inside the human heart."

"You shady bitch; when Lindsay finds out you did this...."

Without delay Passive grabbed her long, pointy machete out of her machete case from behind her leather jacket and beheaded her like it was the medieval times before she could even finish her last sentence. Subsequently, Passive used her blade to carve little s' all over Liz's dead body and mocked her last words. *You shady bitch when Lindsay finds out you did this…. I want that bitch to know I did this duh.*

Reaching inside her black Louie bag, Passive grabbed her black spray can, shook it up, and began spraying the word ***Smoke*** over every single wall in that place while Elvia dealt with Corset.

Soon as Elvia feasted her giant, slanted eyes on Corset, she let two bullets out of her .44 Remington chamber. One for the right temple and one for the left temple and Corset collapsed like building blocks. Elvia put her gun up and stepped over Corset's body to find Passive redecorating Liz's house with the name ***Smoke.***

"Passive here you go with that bullshit. Their dead, now let's go! This is not preschool why you scribble scrabbling on they pale ass walls."

"I'm not dittoing, scribble scrabbling or none of that elementary shit. The word ***Smoke*** means something to me and trust me it's going to mean something in the long run just watch and see. This is exactly why I like to do things by myself. I never have to worry about a little birdie on my shoulders complaining every five seconds."

"If you keep making me feel unappreciated, I promise you I'm going to let your ass hang with the snakes."

"This wasn't no pop-up visit we planned this."

"And your art project wasn't included in the plan!"

"I'm done now Elvia damn! Let's go." And just like that Passive executed her mission with Elvia and made sure that Lindsay was going to reap what she had sewn into existence. Maybe next time Lindsay would learn to keep her claws off of her man.

Bitches be like I'm shady so shady that I kidnapped your man. And I be like I'm shady so shady that I killed your lousy ass mother and your molly maid in her own house under your nose. And I'm so shady that I'm at the 50 yard line and this is the kickoff of my hit-list. I bet you

never had anybody you was beefing with keep you on your

toes like this.

Chapter 6:

Sinful Laxity

I didn't respect you then, and I don't respect you now.....

Out of nowhere Passive's doorbell echoed through her noiseless, companionless house. She started to ignore it, but then she would probably miss out on some entertainment for the day. With her gun on her hip, she didn't even check the blinds; she just went straight for the gusto. And when she opened the door, she practically fainted. It was Smoke's uninvited and unwelcome so called mother Andrea.

What the hell is this lady doing on my doorstep? She ain't never been to my house a day in her motherless life. I don't want to talk to nobody, I don't want to see nobody, and I don't need nobody to help me find my husband or the bitch that kidnapped him. I wish people would just leave me alone and act like they did before any of this shit ever happened.

"Well, if it isn't the unfit mother who abandoned her three kids for a nigga."

"Greetings to you to Passive, I know we haven't always got along, but it really isn't the time or place for whatever issues you may have with me."

"Like hell it isn't. When have we ever got along? When have you ever came around? I'm surprised you even know my name."

"I know I have made some bad decisions, but I know everything that goes on in my kid's lives."

"Your kids are grown, what makes you think they need your useless ass now? Trust me their lives are already fucked."

"Look you little snappy bitch. I am still your mother-in-law so show me some respect! My son is out here somewhere with a psychopath and all you want to do is argue with me?"

"I got everything under control Andrea so you can go back to Vegas or wherever you came from. Matter fact why don't you go visit Omani because you're going to be a grandmother soon."

Then all of a suddenly a teenage girl showed herself from the other side of Passive's doorsteps.

"Passive please we came all the way from Las Vegas to help you," the teenage girl spoke up.

"Let me introduce you. Passive this is my husband's daughter Zana and Zana this is my son's wife Passive."

"You got to be kidding me. So you can take care of your husband's kids, but you couldn't take care of your own kids Andrea?"

"I'm sorry Zana this has nothing to do with you, but this has everything to do with Andrea. Goodbye Andrea," Passive slammed and locked her door in disgust.

"I tried Zana I guess we'll just have to get a hotel room and figure something out," Andrea told Zana.

"I hope you don't give up like you always tell me."

Andrea had a batch of things that she wanted to share with Passive like some of the letters that Smoke had written her over the years before Passive, and everything revolving around Passive until Smoke was kidnapped. It was not Passive's judgment to decide whether Andrea was a good mother or not because the past was the past and presently Andrea had hardcore evidence that would definitely enlighten her daughter-in-law's bitterness against her. Andrea had already put a red ribbon around five of the letters her and Smoke shared so she just slid the letters in the mailbox. Silently praying to herself, Andrea hoped that Passive would come around and they could have a mature conversation together with no profanity or bashing

Pause:

After Andre abandoned his kid's mother/one of the love's of his life/the woman he was about to marry stranded on the curbside of the Las Vegas Beltway in 2003, Andrea wasn't even sweating her freeway heartbreak. She just dusted off her shoulders and started hitch hiking her way to civilization.

If Andre was the only one who thought he had a trick up his sleeve he was sadly fallacious because Andrea had a trick up her wily sleeves also. A woman knows when her man is cheating. Since Andre had his side-piece, Andrea got her a side-piece too. Given that Andrea's ex-boyfriend Zay had attempted to reach out to her a couple of times via postal express, she figured she would write him back. Ultimately, Andrea and Zay became four page letter lovers. When Andrea told Zay who was a prisoner at the Southern Desert Correctional Facility that she was going to be coming to Las Vegas of course Zay wanted Andrea to come visit him. Zay promised Andrea if she moved to Vegas permanently and dropped Andre like a bad habit then she was going to be set for life. Zay was serving a lifelong incarceration sentence for robbery resulting in death. He had plenty of doe saved up from all of the people and the places he robbed. And he was willing to put all of his belongings, his jaw-dropping townhouse, and his Lexus truck all in her itching hands if she finished raising Zay's daughter Zana like she was her own who was 3 years old at the time.

Hell, Andrea didn't even like kids, nor did she raise her own little three bastards, but I guess the chemistry of money and luxury equals a done deal. Andrea was dreading raising a toddler into a woman, but what else was she doing with her time or life anyway. Here it is, a man was voluntarily volunteering to take care of her forever and ever until there was no ever. How could she refuse? Soon as Zana turned 18, she was shipping that ass off to an out-of-state university and putting Zana in a college dorm. Thanks to her father, Zana would have the best education money could buy, but every since she was three and her daddy was locked down, Zana was staying with one of his female workers Saline. And Zay refused to leave his baby girl with a street employee. Unfortunately, Zana's mother died giving birth to her so Zana didn't have a mother figure, but Saline agreed to keep Zana temporarily until Zay found somebody else who would be more suitable for the long-haul.

Once Andre started hinting around he was going to take Andrea to Vegas she knew what time it was. Her ruse was to keep good and silent until her and Andre made it all the way to Vegas then after that she was going to pop-off like a fire-cracker, end the relationship, and walk off. Coincidentally, Andre handled her dirty work for her so all she had to do was land her a ride to Zay so she could get all the confidential information she needed to know in person which was the safest way for them to communicate.

As Andrea was hiking up the road, she was approached by a black heavy duty F-350 truck.

"I usually don't pick up strays, but you look like you can use a ride," a female yelled out of her driver window.

Tired of walking in the hot sun Andrea figured she would take this young lady who looked like she was in her twenties up on her offer.

"Where you headed miss lady?"

"I'm trying to get to Southern Desert Correctional Facility."

"And you thought you was going to get there walking?"

"It's a long story."

"Well we can swap stories on the way."

"Since your kind enough to give me a ride I guess that's the least I can do. I was on my way to marry the love of my life in Vegas when he told me to accept the fact he had another woman. I refused so he put me out, and now

I'm here with you, but I was going to dump him anyway. Two can play that game honey."

"I hear that. What's your name foxy lady?" The driver asked Andrea.

"Andrea and what's yours?"

"Avril."

"Well me and my two home girls just got finished robbing a bank, but don't worry this is not the get-away vehicle, so I felt like blessing somebody since I just indulged in some sinful behavior."

"I'm the last person to judge anybody and I'm not that much of a saint myself so your good with me."

Following 45 minutes of driving, Andrea was at the humble place she needed to be.

"You here ma."

"Thanks for the ride."

"For show here's my number if you need anything, I mean anything just hit me up."

"Will do Avril."

Andrea had never visited anyone in a federal prison, but if she wanted to keep things tight with Zay she didn't have a choice, but to get use to it. Besides, this was one prison visit that was going to change her whole entire life the very moment she stepped foot right inside of those tall, heavily guarded, security gates.

Play:

Now Zana was 14 years old and Andrea and Zana actually had an inseparable, flawless mother-daughter relationship. As much as Andrea claimed to dislike children, she was deeply attached to Zana. Andrea honestly felt remorse for abandoning her kids for a no good nigga, but it was never too late to mature so she tried reaching out to all of her kids and the only person that reached back was her dear son Smoke. At least, somebody forgave her. Maybe her other two children would forgive her also; it would just take them some time. This time around Andrea wasn't going to give up; she was going to try and try and try until she couldn't try no more.

Both Andrea and Zana were living it up in Zay's immaculate townhouse, driving Zay's Lexus truck, blowing money fast because they had it like that. Even while Zay was locked up he was still doing numbers. And the three of them were a strong trio because Andrea made sure Zana visited her daddy every other week, and she wrote him letters once a week.

The sun had definitely been shining in Andrea's life, but now it was the rain.

Chapter 7:

No Filters

Real bitches don't need filters….

Lurking for any small inkling that Passive could acquire to pass by time, Passive did because sleeping, snoring, and dreaming was mostly diminished from her life. Since nothing was the same, Passive only checked the mail once a week. No mailbox check this week so Passive stepped on the porch and pushed the lid up on her black mailbox so she could grab a handful full of what she knew would be junk mail. Flipping through the mail, Passive came across the stack of letters that Andrea left in her mailbox. *These letters were addressed to Andrea Mitchell? So all this time Smoke was going behind my back and writing his mother? Why didn't he just tell me that he wanted to talk to his mother? I do not understand why he did this because it wasn't like that bitch was in jail for child abandonment or something. I mean really did he think I was going to divorce him or something that would be petty as hell?*

Passive kicked and locked her front door closed, untied the ribbon, and pulled one letter out.

March 2012

Dear mom,

I just want to tell you that I am by far the luckiest man on Earth. I am so thankful that I met Passive Boone who is now Passive Boone Mitchell. I can't wait for you to meet her whenever that may be. And yes, we are now married, and don't trip because nobody got an invitation. We had a stress-less, private ceremony at the clerk's office downtown on the international day of happiness which is March 20. Passive did want a huge wedding, but the tragic loss of her father changed her mind. Simplicity was all that mattered at the end of the day since her father wouldn't be able to walk her down the long white aisle. I let her keep her maiden name in remembrance of her father's legacy who was killed before our wedding. So I'll leave the big, magnificent wedding up to one of my sisters. Who knows maybe when we decide to renew our vows we'll have a real, grand ceremony.

Right now we are on our honeymoon and this vacation is everything. I never really got a chance to travel the world as a kid, but as a man I plan to travel everywhere with my wife right by my side. I swear Loyalty should have been her middle name, but since she doesn't have a middle name I'll just pretend that it's Loyalty.

Please tell me how's everything been going for you in Vegas? I know you told me that you reunited with your ex-boyfriend Zay. I know he's behind bars, but I just hope he treats you better then my dad did. And I hope you haven't become a gambler why you sitting around all those casinos.

Love,

your son Smoke

PS. *Don't forget to frame my wedding picture mom!*

In disbelief, Passive threw the letter across the living room. Even though, she knew paper wasn't going to go far it was just the point of her umbrage. On one hand, this letter made Passive fall in love with Smoke all over again, and on the other hand, the concealment made her despise him. *All this time I thought that Smoke hated his mother so I hated her too. I thought that they didn't have any type of relationship or communication, but now this paper trail shows differently. Why baby why? I would've never condemned you for this. I follow your suit and you lead. Whatever enemy you have is mines, whatever friend you have is mines no matter how I feel. Long as nobody disrespects me or our relationship you know I'm good. Now I then cussed this lady out when I should've given her a chance. But look what Omani did when I gave her a chance. How do I know all your family ain't the same? I don't have any children so who am I to criticize another woman about her children? Thank you and no thank you Smoke for showing me something new about you and the wonderful man you are, but please no more surprises.*

Passive had to snap out of it though. Subsequent to a hunch, Passive decided to go to the parking facility at the 11th precinct. Something told her this was the last place Smoke was before he hit the e-way to rescue her. Standing alongside the structure's wall, she was trading glances with her motorcycle, and a sky. All of a suddenly, an unknown car came screeching through the parking structure ramps. Feeling interrupted Passive ran to her motorcycle, jumped on it, and took off as this same random car proceeded to chase her. Switching lanes, hitting corners, and running lights there was no escaping this strange car. Gaining on Passive, this car was really trying its hardest to knock her off of the road. Passive was at loss for words wondering what enemy of hers or Smoke's this was?

I'm absolutely sure Lindsay wouldn't play possum with me in the midnight hours so who the fuck is this?

Next thing Passive knew another motorcycle was gaining on her, but to her reprieve, it was Elvia.

"How did you find me?"

"Everybody has ghosts Passive and four eyes are better then two. I told you I know everything about you."

"So who is this ghost?"

"Your ghost is Shania." Still driving like two bats out of hell, Passive let that name sink into her memory bank.

"You're talking about the tramp that used to work at the 11th precinct with Smoke and kept making passes at him?"

"Ding you got it."

"So what's her beef with me?"

"Passive we can clarify all of this later. Get your face out of the wind and go handle that bitch."

One step ahead of Shania's game, Passive darted out of traffic and started navigating herself through the back roads. Shania had no idea that Passive had somebody working aside her. After hitting a couple of back streets, Passive was speeding up on Shania from behind so Passive pulled out her gun and let four rounds out; one for each of Shania's tires and like always Passive never missed. Losing tire traction, Shania lost control of her vehicle. Instinctively, Shania hit the emergency brake causing her vehicle to do a 360 in the middle of 7 Mile Rd, but since it was late as hell, Shania's car didn't hit anything or anybody.

Still ready to kill Passive, Shania got out of her car and started switching her hips towards Passive. It was like a face-off. Passive was facing Shania and Shania was facing Passive.

"I see Smoke taught you how to shoot, but did Smoke teach you how to fight too?"

"I don't have time to fight no bitch. I'm going to kill you and keep it pushing, but first tell me why you got beef with me?"

"Your husband tried to kill me twice. I've been looking around for him, but since he's seemed to have fallen off the face of the Earth, I knew I would find you."

Fed up with the obvious unnecessary chatting, Elvia rode her bike around Passive and shot Shania in the head.

"Now that bitch is definitely dead and she is not coming back to life after that. And as for you Passive, get your hard-headed ass on your bike and let's go. I told you I would answer all of your questions later. Damn we need to go drop these bikes off and lay low."

"I had everything covered."

"You didn't even know who the bitch was at first. That bitch could've start pulling knives from her coochie on your ass, stabbed you, and then shot you over some damn questions."

"That's what you think."

"That's what I know. You kill everybody Passive then you ask questions later. The last thing we need is this bitch trying to kidnap Smoke or disrupt us finding him."

Everybody knows Passive hated it when she was wrong, but Elvia made a bunch of valid points and that's exactly why Passive kept her mouth shut and rode off in the twilight to Elvia's place.

At Elvia's place, her and Passive cracked open a bottle of Carlo Rossi Moscato Sangria which was the best wine flavor ever invented.

"So tell me what you know about this Shania chick?"

"I know Lindsay hired her to break up your marriage with Smoke and Lindsay pulled some strings to get her into the 11th precinct. Of course that bitch didn't have any police credentials. Lindsay sent that guy I told you about Reno to kill her in the hospital when she was hospitalized, but he shot the wrong target. I don't think you know it, but Smoke drugged Shania the last attempt he made to steal drugs before you got kidnapped, and that's what caused her to be hospitalized. After she was released she tried to tell Smoke the truth about everything, but Smoke snapped on her and cut her ears off. As a result, she had to get some reconstruction surgery, and I guess since she had burnt all of her bridges, she only felt it was right to go after the people who caused her to burn her bridges anyway which was you, Smoke, and Lindsay."

"Talk about detail; I'm still not quite understanding how you know all of this."

"For starters I use to work for Lindsay so I know everything about her whole operation from the people she hired to go after you and Smoke, to the way she does business. I research everything and everyone and keep tabs on everybody around me. I was raised by a hit woman so I have a calculated way of thinking."

Beep. In the mist of Passive's and Elvia's conversation, Passive got a text message notification.

From: (Passive's neighbor)

a bunch of men on motorcycle things just terrorized your house

Passive replied:

thank you for looking out I'll be there shortly

Without delay, Passive and Elvia jumped in Passive's car and sped to her house. Passive's neighbor Audi was always looking out. Since Smoke was the police, her neighbor never called 911 when anything went down in their neighborhood, she just called Smoke. Noble neighbors' lookout, but they mind their own damn business also and that's exactly what Audi did.

I know my motherfucking house better be in one peace or else Gab and all of his cronies are never going to be able to wish or hope again.

When Passive pulled up to her house she was in awe. Apparently, this was the Monarch's retribution day and they did a job on her house. All of the front windows in her house had been busted out completely with no glass left dangling in the window casings. Her front door was snatched off the hinges and rundown. Her lawn was full of clothes, jewelry, tissue, and fine china. Her living room sofa set was parked in the middle of the street with all type of knife stabs, feathers flying like doves, and tire skid marks everywhere. The inside of her whole house had been vandalized from top to bottom. It looked like a blackout mixed with a white house. All of her belongings and hard earnings were broken, destroyed, missing, and mangled like the Monarchs savaged their motorcycles through her house. Elvia didn't have a clue what to say or what Passive was thinking.

I guess this is my karma for all the shit I've been doing lately, but everybody who I have retaliated against deserved it. This is some bitch ass shit here and it makes no sense. Gab must've figured out it was me who was racing him. I'm glad he figured that shit out. I'm shocked that he would do something like this to my house doe knowing Smoke. I'm sure he doesn't know anything about Smoke's disappearance. He probably felt like Smoke sent me to do his dirty work so he sent his biker gang to bark back. And it's cool nobody can hold me down. He's the one lying up in a hospital bed. If this was The Monarch's best then let the games begin because Diamond's best would not get a rebuttal next time around.

"You can stay at my house Passive until we do something about all of this."

"I'm not leaving my house like this Elvia, you can leave if you want too, but I'm not. They touched Smoke's belongings which is the worst thing that anybody could do to a woman in my shoes. They done fucked with the wrong bitch. "

"They fucked with the wrong two bitches you mean. We're in this together so if you want to start cleaning up some of this shit right now, we can get to cleaning right now. And don't stress yourself at all we're going to get them back for this. Right now we need to concentrate on getting Smoke back and when he comes back that will be the best revenge."

Where had friends and women been like Elvia all of Passive's friendless life? That was definitely the realest and kindest shit that a female had ever said to Passive.

"Let's get to cleaning then Elvia." So Elvia and Passive cleaned and cleaned until they were stinking and sweating. When the work morning hit, Passive made all the necessary calls she needed to make to fix this wretched ass

house so Elvia and Passive just sat and chilled there until

all the work was done.

Chapter 8:

Bloody Mary

Trust is something that should never be taken lightly.

The time was near for British to do her routine visit with her dying, inconsolable grandmother. When British tried her key, she realized that the back door was already unlocked so she assumed somebody must've left it unlocked for her. It was no biggie to her. Her grandmother lived in a secure enough vicinity for her to leave her door unlocked 24 hours a day, 7 days a week if she wanted too.

"Grandma! Corset! Anybody home?" British began to get butterflies in her ab-tight stomach when she started getting the feeling that nobody was home.

As British strolled in further and further into her grandmother's space, she got a whiff of death. She stumbled upon Corset whose face was pacific blue with no pulse, she was dead. And British just stepped over her like she was deadweight.

"Too bad she's gone now, she was going to be my maid too, but I guess I'll just find another maid, a younger maid, but none of her blood better not be on my Red

Bottoms." Out of nowhere British hurried up and did a shoe check, right foot then left foot, and no blood was on either shoe so she continued on.

"I'm starting to feel like I'm in a scary movie. I just hope the killer doesn't just jump out and kill me too," British spoke to herself.

Still casual, British swayed up the stairs with her knockoff Birkin bag dangling from her elbow. When she saw her grandmother mutilated, with no pulse, whose face was Atlantic blue, and was dead too, she shut her eyes and rotated her body in the opposite direction. Once British re-opened her murder-filled eyes, she faced the walls, and saw that they were graphitized with the word *Smoke*.

"Is this some sick, twisted joke or something?" British screamed trying to keep hope alive, but nothing about murder was a joke especially not this murder. Not these two, peculiar murders.

British ran to the outskirts of the house to call 911 so she could get those bodies in body bags, proper burials, get an investigation started, and get all that blood and death out of her spirit so she could hurry up and move in and get all of her inheritances too, but first thing first she had to call her man Rue and let him know the good news.

"I was just thinking about you baby, "Rue lied trying to gig British up.

"I got good news baby," British smirked.

"What good news you got?"

"My grandmother is dead and her maid is too so now baby we can get all of my inheritances!"

"Wait, how did that happen? Did you kill them for daddy?"

"No Rue what the fuck is wrong with you? I never killed anyone. I just walked in the house and found both of them dead. Now I'm going to call you back after I deal with the police because I need to call 911."

"Why the fuck didn't you call 911 then instead of calling me?"

"Let's be clear you know damn well I don't give a fuck about nobody, but myself and you. Family don't mean shit to me, I saw an opportunity to get some money and I took it so later baby."

Moments after British hung up with her man, she busted out twerking in the middle of the street like she was auditioning for a strip joint except nobody was watching her rhythmic gyrating. She twerked a little bit for her new finances, she twerked a little bit for her new house, and she twerked a little bit for her new car. She was proud to be an opportunist, and even prouder that her opportunism was finally going to give her the stable life that she always wanted with Rue.

The only person that British dreaded telling about Liz's murder was her daughter Lindsay so British debated with herself up and down Liz's sidewalk.

"Should I tell her or should I let her find out on her own? It ain't like that bitch could care that much anyway because if she did she wouldn't have let this happen. So fuck it. I don't fuck with that bitch anyway and that bitch doesn't fuck with me. She'll find out when she finds out. Oh yeah I forgot that bitch is like an outcast when it comes to family too. "

Upon twenty minutes of British having self-talk with herself finally came the police and an ambulance. The Detroit murdered body count was always increasing so much that the cops surrounding British were in and out of her way like a cable technician. They only asked a few questions, wrote down a few little remarks on a yellow sketch pad, and got the hell up out of dodge. Instantly, British's nipples hardened like she had just participated in a wet t-shirt contest and her black laced Victoria Secret's panties were becoming moist. It was time to celebrate and what a better way to celebrate then to copulate.

Stripping down to her blemish free olive skin, British went to the closest bathroom, took a naked selfie, and sent it to Rue. The caption line said **come get some right now**.

Rue responded instantly: go-figure I'm omw

Whenever his punani called, Rue always I mean always came literally and physically because out of all the bitches he fucked he was use to weak throated bitches and bitches whose cooters just drizzled. British knew how to make her vajizzle squirt seven different ways, and was the most spontaneous sex partner he ever had. Rue loved not having to ask for sex whenever his urges were high. Rue barely had to do shit in the bedroom, but encourage British to control her PC muscles, practice her Kegel exercises, and make her pink canoe tap-out.

Since the guest room was in good shape and nobody was murdered there that's where the bedroom volcano was about to erupt. Ten minutes into British playing patty cake with her clitoris and her vertical clit ring came a few manly knocks at the door. Of course it was Rue whose dick was bulging out of his True Religion jeans and ready to enter British's lethal throat. Sucking dick was all about deep-throating, timing, hand-mouth coordination, sucking everything, and swallowing a little sprinkle, but since British and Rue had sex on the regular he just wanted to feel her jaws wrapped around his shaft before he jammed his Anaconda in her cigar box. After a couple of deep thrusts to stimulate her g-spot, some clit massaging, and some random pulling out, the squirting was on.

"Mm… ah….MMM….YEAH YEAH Right THERE!" British screamed as she squirted like a kitchen faucet with a broken pipe and Rue loved every single moment of it. When he came the two engulfed in each other's arms briefly, but as always Rue had to get back to the streets.

"Our new place is dope shorty I love it," Rue gave British a peck on the cheek. It was actually his first time ever being inside British's grandmother's house as many times as he dropped British off and picked British up.

"You finish getting everything squared away like you always do and I'll see you later." The kiss goodbye was golden, and Rue's happiness made British even happier so nothing could possibly steal her joy.

$

Unfortunately, the fact that Passive still had to make amends with Smoke's mother was still on the floor. Some things in Passive's house were still unfixable, but the major outside blemishes were fixed being her front door, her windows, and a cleaning crew made her hardwood floors spotless. Passive had to 86 a lot of shit in her house, but materialistic shit was always being replaced anyway so it wasn't no biggie. Now Passive was going to have to restrict herself and any visitors from her house like it was a dope house. Even though, Passive and Smoke had an handful of real estate properties, none of their properties were secure with the possibility of an unpredictable motorcycle alliance gang banging them. So staying at Elvia's house was definitely not a bad idea. Never in Passive's mind would she have thought that her and Elvia would become as thick as thieves, but they were. And Elvia parlayed with Passive the whole time like a true friend.

"Elvia, I know I probably came off as a bitch too you, but it's for good reason. I must say I never had any friends so having a friend like you is everything."

"Passive I never had any friends either growing up. All I had was Posh, so I do appreciate every bit of our friendship, partnership, or sisterhood. I hope nothing ever comes between us."

"And I know I said when Smoke comes back our friendship would be over, but I want us to remain friends."

"You took the words right out of me."

"I hate to admit it, but I owe Smoke's mother an apology and since I can't meet with her at my house would it be okay if I met with her at your house?"

"Yeah that's cool just set it up and make it happen."

"Since Smoke has been gone I've been finding out all type of things about him that I never ever knew. I can't call them secrets because I don't see it that way. I just see them as misunderstandings that need to be discussed. I blame myself because like I said I have a shitty attitude at times."

"Everybody puts up walls Passive, and the people that don't are the people who should. You just have to know when to take those walls down, but only you have the power to be the judge of that like you are. As women we go through so many things, and trust is something that shouldn't be taken lightly."

Damn, Elvia talked so inquisitively and that's a big reason why I love talking to her. I had somebody to watch my back, mixed with somebody who I could learn from, and somebody who could give me criticism that I could accept. Elvia's astuteness was sexy as hell because I always thought most women were either gullible or just dumb.

Chapter 9:

Trouble in Paradise

Who sank the love boat?

Back in Missouri, under the Missourian law radar was Paradise. Sweet, old, nasty love brought her over 1,000 miles from where she was hiding with the loot she ripped off of Smoke and Passive. She was in love with the Michael Kors promises, and Neiman Marcus shopping binges she always got when she visited him. She only wanted "him" to detonate the cream in the middle of her milky way. She was tired of imagining pleasure, and co-pleasuring herself. She missed her partner in crime Champagne a little bit, but not nearly as much as she missed "him."

Never did Paradise have mutual intentions with Champagne when it came down to investing their stolen money. Champagne wanted drugs and Paradise just wanted the commodity of money. Apparently, two shades of greed, and two desperate women trying to make a quick come up didn't mix.

"I'm downstairs baby."

Feeling like she just hit the mega-millions, Paradise grabbed her purse, checked herself in the mirror, and ran out of the door.

Soon as she spotted a black luxury town car that resembled all the black luxury town cars Cahill Ceasar rode in, she sashayed to it, sprung open the back door, and hopped in. Paradise immediately kissed her man like she was kissing him for the first time.

"I see you missed me."

"You damn right I missed you." Cahill smacked and squeezed Paradise's ass.

"So you still haven't told me why you had to leave Missouri in the first place." Cahill didn't have a clue that his woman was an accessory to kidnapping, and attempted robbery of drug money so Paradise as usual just made up some shit to quiet her boo.

"I've been in Missouri all my life and I'm just ready for a change so I called myself trying to relocate."

"Well my job has moved me to Missouri so whatever life crisis you are having you can swallow it, because I need you here with me unless you want to be replaced."

"I don't ever want to lose you bay so I guess Missouri it stays." In all honesty, Paradise didn't want to be nowhere near Missouri or its state lines, or its surrounding states, but she couldn't risk losing Cahill. He was too rich, he worked for the government, and she was his woman. Life couldn't possibly get any magnificent then what life was like with him.

There was something that Cahill forgot to tell Paradise, and when they woke up together and he was stroking her back he remembered.

"Paradise have you heard about your friend? Is that why you don't like it here in Missouri anymore?"

"What friend bay I don't know what your talking about?"

"Your friend Champagne was found murdered?"

"Why haven't you been told me about this Cahill?" Paradise started to get upset and alarmed.

"It was your friend I thought somebody would've told you by now. I barely have time to talk to you on the phone or see you, but my time with you is all about you and nobody else so watch who you checking."

"I'm sorry I just don't know how to handle bad news like that," Paradise pretended to be sympathetic, but she was really getting nervous because if Champagne was dead that meant Paradise's life was on the line too. Something could've gone wrong with the kidnapping, or somebody could've come to rescue the kidnapped girl, or the mastermind behind the whole Passive scheme could've murdered everybody at that house, it could be a number of things. Even though, Paradise agreed to stay in her hometown with Cahill, how was she going to explain that she had a bounty hit out on her head to him? She knew he had a bad temper, but she didn't know what kinds of horrific things he did in the dark or in his past. None of his women ever left him alive, just like nobody crossed him. It was no way in hell that Paradise was just going to rot in Missouri and die so she decided to run. She had some family in Detroit, MI and money-wise she was set for life. Soon as Cahill left for one of his work-related meetings, Paradise left for the 313.

$

At the bottom of another 4 page letter that Passive ended up reading from Smoke to his mother was Andrea's telephone number. Just as Passive promised herself, she made arrangements for Andrea to come over Elvia's house so the two of them could hash everything out. Passive hadn't cooked in ages, but since she made an ass out of herself by going against the wishes of her husband she had to make-up correctly. Passive read that Andrea's favorite meal was nacho salad so she cooked up some hamburger meat, made a tray full of vegetables, a tray full of Mexican cheeses, laid out the salsa, the sour cream, and made some fresh lemonade to sip on.

Hearing the sound of Elvia's doorbell meant that Andrea had made it, her and Zana. Instantly, the Mexican aromas hit Andrea's nostrils and she was proud to be Passive's mother-in-law.

"Passive you made my favorite dish?" Passive gave Andrea a warm hug and Zana.

"I did make your favorite dish. Don't ask me how I knew just know I pay attention to detail so let's eat and then talk."

"Well I don't mean to be nosy, but whose house are we dining at?"

"My sister from another mother Elvia, she's giving us privacy right now so I'll introduce you to her on a later date. Since we're asking questions, who is Smoke's cousin Gab in relationship to you?"

"Cousin Gab is my nephew why you ask?"

"Gab and his motorcycle gang terrorized my house and that's why I'm here. And when I say terrorized I mean my house is an atrocity now on the inside because of all my damaged goods. He got mad because I beat him in a motorcycle race and I won Smoke's bike back from him. Did Smoke ever tell you about the incident that happened between them?"

"Thank you for sharing that with me and Smoke did tell me about how Gab basically stole his bike. Don't worry about it I'll take care of it," Andrea affirmed that quick and easy like she was an undercover gangster too.

Both Andrea and Zana ended up getting seconds and drinking all the fresh lemonade Passive had made which meant that Andrea and Zana were certainly going to be team Passive now. Since their stomachs were full, it was time to get down to the real nitty, gritty.

"Andrea, please let me start off by apologizing for my behavior when you came to my house, and let me apologize to you Zana for even allowing you to hear me disrespect your mother like that."

"I forgive you Passive, you were only doing what you thought was right. I can tell that you really love my son, and I am so grateful for that."

"It's okay Passive, but now we can all make-up so we can be a real family. I always wanted a big sister."

"So Andrea, how did you know that Smoke was in trouble besides him not writing you?"

"My husband Zay is in prison so he hears everything and he heard about Lindsay Chambers. I guess her magazine made it through the prison system too so all the cellmates would be exchanging stories about you. Zay knows that you are Smoke's wife and Omani is my daughter so he started paying extra attention to conversations after that issue surfaced with you and Omani.

If you remember Chill, he got caught up in some mess in Vegas and winded up becoming cellmates next to Zay. He told Zay about how Lindsay had got you kidnapped in Missouri and had kidnapped Smoke which led Zay to telling me. I had to come here and see for myself so I did. A mother can feel when her child is in trouble, and I feel it. It's not a good feeling at all."

"So y'all have been communicating all these years?"

"Yes we have, Smoke took that upon himself as my oldest, and the overseer of his sisters. And I admire him for that even though I messed up terribly as a mother you live and you learn. I don't know where you got your ammunition from, but girl you blasted the shit out of me that day," Andrea laughed.

"Yes as you can tell I have my way with words, but some of my ammunition comes from fear and a little bit of jealousy. I have a big fear of letting people in because I've been hurt so many times by the people that I love the most. Neither me nor Smoke had suitable relationships with our mothers being that you left him, and my mother was killed. It has always been just me and Smoke which is the safest thing that I knew. And I had fear that after knowing you I would actually love you and then you would hurt me too. I just wasn't ready to love another woman as my mother, because I still haven't gotten over the fact of my mother being killed. Her murder was never solved and I have a gut feeling about who did it which is why I can't let her murder go."

"I can understand all of that so who do you think killed your mother?"

"I have reason to believe my father's best friend killed both my mother and father."

"That must've been some powerful man if he had it out for both of your parents. And if you think he did it I'm sure he did it."

"Yeah and the sad part about is he is supposed to be an iconic person. I'm sure you heard of him. He was the mayor of Detroit once upon a time. His name is Cahill Ceasar."

"Passive no, not a dirty government trashbag?"

"Yes and something is telling me we're going to collide again. But off of that, I just want you to know that I won't sleep until I get your son back so you can count on that. You can forget all about writing him. I'm going to make sure you see him in the flesh."

"Thank you Passive for everything. Me and Zana are going to get going and we'll be in touch."

Chapter 10:

Mrs. Officer

You have the right to remain silent...

Gossip spread like a weather cold front all the way from Detroit, MI precinct chalkboards to Marcela's Louisville's home in Kentucky. Apparently, two of her family members had been murdered within the last week; Novara Chambers- her cousin and Liz Chambers- her father's ex-wife and her step sister's mother and police authorities felt these gruesome murders were connected. Even though Liz wasn't Marcela's biological mother, family was family whether it was by marriage, law, or association. Anybody that was in her father's life was in her life also, and since her father wouldn't miss his ex-wife's funeral, Marcela wasn't going to miss it either. Being that Marcela had a friend who served on the Detroit Police force, Marcela was desperate to pay him another visit so she hopped on the next plane west to Detroit, MI. Somebody had to play detective for this family.

Her first stop after she landed was the 11th precinct once again. Gliding through the police doors, Marcela headed for the reception desk.

"Yes I would like to see Captain Smoke Mitchell."

Lucky for Marcela, Officer Rodgers was working the reception desk and remembered Marcela's face from the last time she visited the department. Otherwise Team Smoke would've let a good plug go astray.

"What is your name ma'am?"

"Marcela Chambers."

"Okay follow me in the back and don't talk to anyone else about why your here, but if anyone asks you tell them Officer Rodgers is assisting you." Marcela didn't know what type of protocol or undercover bullshit was going on today, but all she could do was sit, wait, and hope that Smoke came through for her like he always did.

"Most def no problem." Once Rodgers got Marcela cozy in an interrogation room, he snuck away to call

Passive, and Passive answered every call from the precinct on the first ring.

"Hello, this is Mrs. Mitchell?"

"Passive, how quick can you come to the station?"

"Ten minutes or less what's popping Rodgers?"

"This woman is here by the name of Marcela Chambers, and she has visited Smoke before, and she is asking to visit him again. I didn't brief her in on anything. I just took her to a room, and I'm calling you, but I'm sure she knows something so how do you want to handle this?"

"I'll be there pronto, just keep her relaxed until I get there, and then I'll take things from there."

"You got it Mrs. Mitch see you in a minute."

Passive freshened up, grabbed her motorcycle, and hit the station. On the way there she couldn't stop thinking to herself. *I wonder what Chamber's branch did this Marcela bitch fall off of and why is she looking for Smoke? And why the fuck is she having pop-up visits with my man?*

It's been too many years for this bitch to still be hanging around Smoke. Maybe this bitch ain't never been in a real relationship or something because Smoke and I don't have friends or outsiders loitering around us. Whatever this bitch agenda is, I'm sure as hell going to find out.

Rodgers was waiting at the back entrance to let Passive in and direct her to the room that Marcela was waiting in. Once Passive was in it was on.

"Hi, how are you doing Marcela, I'm Smoke's wife, Passive and I hear that your looking for my husband?" Passive flashed a fake smile and stuck her hand out to shake Marcela's.

"Is this some type of ambush because I'm not sleeping with your husband or nothing like that if that's what your thinking?"

"I don't know what to think, I'm trying to find out exactly why your here?"

"My mother and my cousin were both murdered here in cold blood and I want Smoke to find out who did it."

"Well, let me ask you a question. What's your relationship to Lindsay Chambers? I'm sure you haven't spoken with her in months."

"What does Lindsay Chambers have to do with this?"

"Just answer the question or am I going to have to get one of these officers to arrest you for withholding information in a criminal investigation?"

"That's not necessary, Lindsay is my sister."

"Your sister kidnapped my husband and now he's missing so if you want him to help you solve your mystery murders, I need you to help me find my husband, and since that's your sister I'm sure your capable of that."

"That's just like snitching, but worst. Why should I risk the loyalty of my sister for this investigation when anybody could've kidnapped him? He's a cop, nobody likes cop. You see cops having funerals every day. Don't try to put that bullshit on my sister!"

"Excuse me for a minute."

Officer Rodgers was nearby a couple of doors down pacing the kitchen floors praying that Marcela could bring back his Captain.

"Rodgers I need you to go to RECORDS and get me the recording of the visit that Smoke had with her right away, and any other documentation from that visit that you have, and give me everything that you got on her, full name, address, close family, businesses, everything!"

Rodgers did exactly what he was told and returned to Passive with everything that she asked for. Skimming through all of Marcela's information Passive found a lot of interesting facts to use against her in rebuttal.

"So what did you find on me?" Marcela asked upon Passive's return just after re-glossing her dry lips.

"It's funny that your trying to front like Lindsay didn't kidnap him, when your last visit here you came here to warn my husband about your sister and how grossly obsessed she is with him still. Not only that, but you were sure that your sister had something to do with a Louisville murder by the name of Julie (June) Harris. As a matter of fact, your sister kidnapped me a couple weeks after June was killed. And she told me herself that she had Smoke in her custody, and implied that she was already making him forget about me. I know she has psychological issues, and I know y'all have a tight bond because your the only sibling that she has, and I know that she has deposited a lot of dirty money into your bank accounts. Ain't no other city cops goin help you and that's exactly why you came here. They're just going to close those cases, label them as gang-related murders, and put them in storage in a file cabinet. You mine as well catch the next plane smoking back to Louisville because your wasting your time here. "

"Do you plan on killing my sister?"

"I rather not answer that question."

"If you want me to help you, I need to know what your intentions are."

"If I have too I will, but honestly I just want my husband back, and then we can lock Lindsay up for all the murders she is responsible for." Lying was played out, but sometimes you had to lie to get what you wanted because Passive knew damn well she was going to bury Lindsay off GP. And even though Passive knew who killed Liz Chambers, and found out that Novara Chambers was the girl who committed suicide when her and Elvia killed Solei, she wasn't ashamed.

"That's fair I guess, so I'm going to call her and set-up a visit with her ASAP. I'm going to tell her it's crucial that I see her face to face, and see if I can find out anything else. Lindsay is like a talking journal over the phone. I'm sure she will tell me everything you need to know. All I have to do is listen."

"And just so I can keep my end of the bargain I advise you to make sure she is nowhere near wherever Smoke is being held when I get there. Why don't you set-up a lunch with her or something, and why y'all have lunch, I will be busting Smoke out. And if you decide to cross me, trust me I got people and they will .22 millimeter your ass."

"I don't want to cross you. Smoke is like a brother to me, and I want my sister's services to be reinstated in somebody's psyche ward." Even though, Marcela claimed she didn't want to cross Passive, Passive knew how quickly bitches flip flopped. Bitches say one thing, then next thing you know their doing another. Not only that, but Marcela was a "Chambers" which meant she was probably born in some loony bucket too and had mental disabilities too so

Passive had to tell her back-up Elvia everything that was emerging, but first Marcela had to make the call.

"Ring, ring..." Lindsay's phone rang for hours before she finally answered it.

"This better be important Marcela."

"The fact that I haven't heard from you in months is not enough? And some terrible things have occurred in our family, we need to meet right away to talk."

"I'm at my cabin in Niagara Falls, Canada."

"What the hell are you doing in Canada Lindsay? I thought you hated your cabin."

"I did hate my cabin, but Darnell and I needed someplace far to go."

"When did you get a boyfriend and who the fuck is Darnell?"

"Don't act like you didn't know Smoke's name was Darnell."

"I forgot that was his legal name. Nobody calls him by that. Why would Smoke won't to be in a cabin, in the middle of nowhere, with you Lindsay?"

"Why wouldn't he? Whatever just call me when you get here so I can meet you somewhere for lunch. I have to get back to my wifely duties."

By the sound of Lindsay's wild confirmations, Passive was righter then right and Lindsay was definitely holding Smoke captive.

"So what's the verdict?" Passive asked hesitant to know.

"Lindsay has a cabin in Niagara Falls, Canada and that's where she's holding Smoke. I'm sorry, but I think she may have married him or something."

"Spare my ears with that bitch wacko ass attempts to steal my husband. I'm going to get my people ready and you get yourself ready because we're bringing Smoke back home tomorrow."

"Passive I just got here in the D today and I haven't even got to visit my mother's house yet. I know you won't your husband back, but damn can I pay my respects to my mother first?"

"Your mother is dead, Smoke is alive, and he is the key to your puzzle. You can pay your respects while we getting everything together, but trust and believe we catching a flight out of here no later than 6AM. So be done with the boo-wooing by 9 o'clock. And remember what I said, don't cross me."

Spoken like a true bitch, it is what it is. *You lost your mother, I lost my husband, and if you want to cry about mothers, I was raised without one so what can you possibly know about being motherless? Marcela better be lucky I said tonight, and not right now because I need Smoke right now, and the closer I get to finding him and too the dusty rag a muffin bitch that stole him from me, the madder I get. I promise you if she has altered or damaged*

138

anything on his torso, I'm going to Kill Bill that bitch and

bury her alive.

Passive shot Elvia a text:

meet me at my house ASAP, we got to go out of

town, c u in a min

Elvia texted back:

I'll be there shortly

Pissed off that her 11th precinct visit was becoming

like a nightmare on Elm Street, Marcela headed for

Lindsay's mother's house. When Marcela got there, it was

U-Haul moving trucks everywhere. Somebody was moving

in Liz's house already, and she hadn't even had a funeral

yet.

"Hello?" Marcela walked in like she lived there.

"Excuse me don't you believe in knocking? British

asked when she caught a glimpse of Marcela.

"If you wanted me to knock you should've locked

your door."

"I don't know you so you can leave and I'll pretend like I never saw you."

"I'm not leaving, but what you are going to do is tell me why your moving into my sister's mother's house when this house should be off the market?"

"My name is over the will, everything is mine including this house so run and tell that bitch you call a sister that."

"Are you sure that's the exact message you won't me to give to Lindsay?"

"You've talked to Lindsay?" British asked switching her whole demeanor.

"I talk to Lindsay every day, I just told you she's my sister, and I know she would blow a gasket if she knew about any of this so I think I should go run and tell that bitch everything that's going on."

"Wait please don't call Lindsay on me. I know it's going to be conflict about me living in her mother's house, but her mother is my grandmother, and I can't help that my grandmother left me with everything. It must be something we can do about this right?"

"There is nothing "we" can do about this. I don't know you, I heard stories about you, but I don't know you. Lindsay is going to find out one way or another whether I tell her or not so enjoy all of this while you can because once she comes back it's going to be hell to pay."

"Tell that bitch to bring it then!"

Marcela exited the house with a for sure way to distract Lindsay at their luncheon while Passive did her thing and rescued Smoke. Methods exist everywhere even for a person who lives in jeopardy.

Chapter 11:

Captivity

You can't hold me hostage forever....

The province of Ontario, Canada was so low-key that if Lindsay wouldn't have leaked her private location to her sister Marcela, nobody's wide nose would've ever discovered her. Hidden in the Branches of Niagara Campground little 15 log cabin community, Lindsay had one of the best cabins on its 70 acres of land. Features included a woodstove style heater, beautiful cedar log furniture, a separate bedroom with a queen bed, a living area with a futon bed, coffee table and chairs, and a staircase leading to a loft with two full size beds and one twin bed. There was a full bath and kitchenette, air conditioning, and her cabin slept six people maximum. Her cabin was only 10 street minutes away from Niagara Falls State Park, and 15 minutes away from the city of Buffalo. What better place to have an excluded cabin then the 7th wonder of the world?

Grand Island, New York on 2659 Whitehaven Road was the precise location of Lindsay Chambers and her hostage Smoke Mitchell.

REWIND:

Lindsay knew off rip that Smoke was going to try to rescue his wife soon as he found out where she was in dismay so she camped out on 1-70 West, pulled over on the fast lane side, and sat in her vehicle staking out Smoke's grey Jaguar XK coupe. Tenaciously, Lindsay flattened two of her tires by just simply unscrewing the valve inside the stem of her tires on the rim and just releasing all the air out. Then she got back in her car and turned on her hazard lights knowing that Smoke was a patron of the law, and even though he had a one track mind at the time, he wasn't going to pass by a broke down vehicle without helping. After a few boring hours of waiting, Lindsay's suppositions of Smoke and his patriotism was correct, because a vanity mirror revealed his grey Jaguar pulling behind her.

In Lindsay's cup-holder was a bottle of chloroform and on the passenger seat was the towel she was going to soak the chloroform in. She had to move promptly because she heard a car door closing which meant Smoke was exiting his vehicle. And the last thing she wanted was for him to recognize her face and getaway before she could trap him. Swiftly, Lindsay made her deadly concoction, opened her door, got out of her vehicle, and bent down in front of her tire like she was doing a tire check.

"I see your tires are flat is somebody on the way to help you?" Smoke asked the stranger approaching Lindsay's vehicle.

"Roadside assistance is supposed to be on their way, but they said that hours ago. I think I have a nail stuck in my tire?" Lindsay lied still bent down at her tire.

"Let me check your tires then." Smoke bent down towards her tires and Lindsay rose up behind him.

"Is it okay if I go sit in your car until somebody gets here?"

"Okay, but please don't touch anything miss."

Lindsay reached in her car, grabbed the towel, and sat in the backseat. When Smoke came back to the car, he didn't understand why the stranger chose to sit in the backseat like she was sitting in a taxi cab or something.

"So what's your plan miss?" Smoke asked sitting back in his seat. It was at that instance when Lindsay reached in the front and smothered Smoke's face with the sleepy hollow towel until he was unconscious. He tried to fight it, but the chemical was too strong. Once Smoke was unconscious she moved his body to the passenger seat and put handcuffs on his arms and his legs. Then she drove off to her private jet she had stationed for them 5 highway minutes away. She left his car by a barn in the middle of the country at an abandoned house, where nobody would notice it because the piece of Missourian property was covered by high, stocky fields. Her jet driver Benjamin helped her maneuver Smoke into the jet and soon as everybody was fastened in they took off.

$

Andrea felt obligated to set the record straight since she now was a certified mother-in-law. Zana was old enough to watch herself so she didn't have to worry about any CPS investigations. The worst thing that could probably emerge is Zana locking herself out of their hotel room. Now that Zana had a big sister maybe she would call her big sister Passive to come help her or ask the hotel clerk to let her in.

Andrea hadn't seen any of her trillion family members since she skedaddled to Vegas, but surprise, surprise because Cajon's mother Carina was about to get a knock at her door.

Knock, knock.

"Hello Carina."

"Oh my god, are you really here? Look at my little sister. I haven't seen you in ages please come in."

"I can't believe you still live at the same house, and on the same block you did 11 years ago."

"Yeah so why have you let 11 years go by without talking to your sister?"

"You know how I feel about family and once I left this forsaken place for Vegas I never came back. I never wanted to come back. This is actually my first time returning since then. I came to find out about my son Smoke; he was kidnapped. Plus I have a daughter-in-law now that resides here, I'm a soon-to-be grandmother from Omani, I live in Vegas now, I married my husband Zay who I use to date back in the day, and I've been caring for his daughter Zana."

"Wow a lot has happened to you, but nothing has changed here. I still work at the Post Office delivering mail and Cajon still lives here. He got into some shit on that damn motorcycle of his and den ended up with a broken femur." Andrea didn't care to talk to her sister because her sister was a drug addict/nothing ass bitch who looked older then Oprah. Dealing with addiction was no hoe and Andrea got tired of doing it. That's exactly why they had a deteriorated ass relationship.

"I need to go holler at him right quick I'll be right back." Trailing through Carina's house most men lived in their mommy's basement so Andrea went straight for it.

"Aunt Andrea didn't anybody tell you to knock before you enter?" Cajon never forget a face as he saw Andrea coming down the stairs. Andrea made her pistol visible to Cajon and laid it flat on his coffee table.

"What did I do auntie why are we pulling out guns?"

"Why the fuck did you and your motorcycle gang trash my son's house?"

"That shit don't have anything to do with you auntie that's official motorcycle business. I can't even talk about that with you." Andrea snatched up her pistol and struck Cajon's casted leg with it until he hollered in writhing pain.

"Passive is my daughter-in-law so that has everything to do with me. Smoke has been kidnapped and I'm telling you now if you and your motorcycle gang don't leave Passive alone I will break every fragile bone in your body. And I'll wipe your motorcycle clique off of the map."

"I wasn't there when they did that so why you mad at me? I thought that girl name was Diamond I didn't know she was family," Cajon lied and told the truth at the same time.

"Your the one that told them to do it so don't try to bullshit me. All I know is that incident your stupid circle did is where this shit ends. Are we clear or do I need to bust a cap in your ass and let you know I'm not playing?"

"We got an understanding."

"We better have an understanding because I could turn your ass into the feds for being a drug dealer. I know your still giving your mother the same drugs that your out here selling."

"That would be some hating shit auntie."

"Don't fucking auntie me call me Andrea. I'm out of here." Andrea left without even telling Carina goodbye. It wasn't like Carina had enough decency to walk Andrea to the door anyway or come see who was walking around her house. All Carina cared about was her drugs, nothing else mattered, not a sister, not a sibling, and not a son.

Chapter 12:

Empire State of Mind

I don't need an army, but I got one...

Posh, Elvia, Passive, and Marcela all made it to the Empire State with their empire state of minds. Being that the four ladies boarded the same Delta Airlines plane at the McNamara Terminal at 5:40 A.M., they all took their flight to have bonding time and plot Operation Smoke precisely. Skeptically, Elvia knew Passive didn't like newcomers, but the severity of this code red situation and the fact that Lindsay's cabin was going to be heavily guarded had Elvia make arrangements for back-up. Being that Elvia had shared many war stories with Passive about Posh, Passive didn't challenge Elvia's decision to bring on Posh.

On the plane, Passive studied Posh especially since this was her first time actually being in her physical presence. Passive's eyes met with Posh's fingers when she noticed a ring glistening more than crystal glass.

"I see your ring shining over here Posh; Elvia didn't tell me that you are married."

"Elvia didn't know, we actually have a lot of catching up to do, but we can catch up after we bring your husband home. Then maybe we all can go on a vacation."

"I haven't been on a vacation in ages. We're definitely going to have to make that happen," Passive visualized herself laying on a island somewhere soaking up some sun in a sexy two-piece bikini.

"So Marcela I'm up-to-date on everything and I pray that you ain't nothing like your sister because if anything I mean anything happens to Elvia or Passive I promise you I will butcher your ass," Posh threatened.

"I really understand why y'all have to threaten me every five seconds, but can I please earn my own credibility. Judge me for being me and not for being Lindsay's sister. Everybody has a part and I am risking more than anybody on this plane. Blood is supposed to be thicker than water, but in this situation I beg to differ."

"Okay Marcela we'll give you a chance, but you better keep our threats in the back, front, and side of your mind," Elvia reminded Marcela.

Since Posh had the most expertise on killing people 101, she was going to be the ringleader of their top secret siege. Marcela was going to text her crew the moment that Lindsay arrived to the restaurant so that Posh and her mob squad could go to work on Lindsay's cabin, and be on the next highway somewhere far away from Lindsay and Ontario. Passive and the girls were going to be staking out in their vehicle close to the premises so they could get an eye for all the surroundings. They needed to know how many guards there were, if there were any other visitors at the other cabins, and they needed to pinpoint their main target cabin.

Posh's husband Corbin just so happened to be taking care of some official business in Buffalo, New York. His two assignments were to pick the girls up from the airport and get a trunk full of artillery from one of his weapon connects. It was going to be two less things that the girls had to do when they landed in the N-Y. Corbin wanted to tag along on Passive's rescue mission so bad, but this was a lady's mission- no men were allowed on the premises so the whole ride to Enterprise-Rent-A-Car Corbin was having a begging frenzy. Marcela needed her own rental car to meet up with Lindsay at the restaurant so she could come and go as she pleased.

"Passive come on now, I know y'all doing the Charlie's Angels thing, but let me assist y'all ladies. I'm familiar with your husband Smoke and from what I can remember he's a real cool cat. We bumped into each other a few times upstate and we always talked about collaborating together, but we just never did it because he was too busy slanging with females. I told him females were going to be the death of him one day, but I see he didn't listen to me."

"I appreciate your concern Corbin, but with all due respect me, your wife, and Elvia got this. They are honestly lucky to be here because I like riding out alone, but I decided it was okay not to be so cocky in this situation so don't push your luck."

"Please Passive?"

"No Corbin!" All the ladies answered in unison.

Pulling off in a McIntosh Apple Red Cadillac ATS, it was 11 AM and Marcela was on the go headed to The Beach House Restaurant in Grand Island, New York to meet up with her very distraught sister. They had to wine and dine at one of the diciest bar and grills in the entire state. Before Marcela set her GPS, she had to make a courtesy phone call.

"What's up sis I made it to New York, I just left the airport. Are we still meeting up for lunch or what?"

"I forgot all about our lunch. How long do you plan on being in New York?"

"How could you forget Lindsay? I haven't seen you in months. I've been looking forward to our lunch since we last talked. I told you I have a lot of shit that needs to be addressed to you ASAP and it cannot wait?"

"Okay damn I get it do you got a spot that you want to meet at? You know how travel savvy you are."

"Yes I won't to go to the Beach House which is not too far away from your cabin so you won't have to travel long. I read some great culinary critiques and reviews about them so I'm anxious to check them out. They got a nice selection of food and some wine so you know I'm there."

"Okay I'll meet you there at 12 so you can do the honors of getting a table for us like you always do."

Immediately Marcela let her crew know that everything was on the go and that Lindsay should be exiting the cabin in approximately 30-40 minutes. The trio was strapped with guns, knives, grenades, bullet proof vests, their Air Jordan mid-tops, black jogging suits, black

Darth Vader sunglasses, and black gloves. Their most important rule was never to leave their fingerprints anywhere whatsoever, and never to take off their gloves. By the looks of the premises the cabin lot had 15 cabins, and there were 3 guards stationed around the middle cabin which must've been Lindsay's main cabin where she was keeping Smoke.

The nick of time was going by slower than a snail walking. The instance their binoculars saw Lindsay up, close, and personal for the first time in all of their shady missions was the same instances that palms got sweaty and emotions got heavy. Lindsay walked to her car so fast you would've thought that she was a real celebrity avoiding some type of paparazzi.

It was about to be time to ride, and a few minutes after Lindsay pulled off the premises in her swagged out black Buick LaCrosse, the group said a silent prayer amongst themselves, and put their Smoke faces on. Like a cold breeze, Posh, Elvia, and Passive each took on an armed guard, sprayed them up with bullets and laid them out. Elvia and Passive went into the cabin while Posh made sure that the premises stayed clear. The outside of the cabin didn't look like it was going to be shit, but the inside of the cabin was decked out. Passive went off searching for Smoke while Elvia made sure that there was no other armed guards hiding inside the cabin. Passive ended up finding her way to Smoke as she made it up to the attic. She saw him in the worst conditions she had ever seen him in his whole entire life.

"Elvia I'm in the attic! Smoke is in the attic! Come up here and help me!" Smoke could see Passive, but he couldn't talk so he kept bobbing his head towards the closet. Passive could read her man like a book so she knew that meant that somebody was waiting in the closet except the joke was on them. They should've came out shooting the moment that they heard Diamond yelling through the attic, and strangers entering the house, but since they wanted to play pussycat then pussycat it was. Diamond opened up the closet doors as a couple of gunshots sounded off from the person in the closet and Diamond's chambers', Diamond was the last bitch standing. After Diamond handled that, Smoke started motioning his head to the corners like there was something else she was forgetting. Apparently, Lindsay's cabin was strapped with hella cameras. *Nope bitch your spying games are over, and so is your sick infatuation with my husband. I told you he was my husband bitch. My last name is Mitchell and I got the ring. You will and can never take my place no matter what shady shit you come up with. By the time you find out Smoke's gone, we'll be long gone.*

"Make sure you ice all the cameras!"

Zooming in on Smoke his appearance was all bad. For somebody to be so madly obsessed with him, by the looks of it Smoke had been going through 500 degrees of hell. His muscles have shrunken to bones like he hadn't eaten in months. *I wouldn't eat anything from a crazy bitch neither because Lindsay would definitely poison somebody.* His facial hair had grown long and thick like Santa Claus beard, and he was practically growing a full-blown afro. There were used condoms and open Magnum condom wrappers everywhere which meant Smoke had been having sex with Lindsay, but Passive knew deep down inside that Smoke would never do that. The sex that Lindsay and Smoke had was forced and not consensual. Just look at how he was being kept and unkept; he had a black leather slave mouth harness on with a ball so all Smoke could do was gag. Lindsay had tied nylon rope tightly around his wrists to a piece of steel post she made near a corner of the attic. Lindsay didn't even have enough decency to tie Smoke up in a bed. She had him setting upright, back against the walls, legs spread out on the floor in a corner like he was in timeout or something. Once Passive got the harness off she

162

had to get his hands loose without poking herself or Smoke with the acupuncture needles Lindsay had stationed on the post. Smoke had a smudge of red lipstick on his left cheek like Lindsay must've kissed him goodbye before she took off. Smoke was dressed in some bummy clothes which included a wife beater and some Adidas jogging pants. And looking at Smoke's right arm appeared a tattoo; a fairly large tattoo that read Lindsay in big, bold, black Old English lettering. After seeing that gruesome mark on his body and all the other exterior nonsense that she had noticed, Passive wanted to relinquish this moment.

I can't believe this bitch then branded my man. I know I told Marcela I wasn't going to kill the bitch, but fuck that I meant I wasn't going to kill the bitch today. Soon as today passes that retarded bitch is going to be on somebody's milk carton for being missing. I got to kill the bitch anyway because if I don't she's never going to stop torturing my family. I will not risk losing Smoke a second

time or anybody else in my life. Life is too short for this
type of sporadic behavior to be occurring and reoccurring.
Somebody has to beat the odds of this bitch so either that
bitch can start festering off somebody else or plan A- I got
to kill her.

Rejoicing in Smoke's return, she was overjoyed he
was back. Even if he wasn't in tip top shape, had some
battle wounds, and some bad memories; he was still her
Smoke. Passive had never missed or loved anyone as much
as she loved and missed Smoke. He was the oxygen in her
lungs, the sun in her sky, and he owned the love that flowed
within her heart. Lindsay was hell, but so were the days
that Passive had to spend without him.

I'll think about killing that bitch later for right now
all I want to do is be thankful for the brazen, incredible
man that I have. All I want to do is be an arm, an ear, a
shoulder, or anything that Smoke needs in this healing
process. I will cater to him in every way possible. If people

thought that Smoke and Passive was something before, then

they should definitely be afraid of the new and improved

Smoke and Passive.

Chapter 13

On the Run

Out of the house of bondage….

Air, wind, and sunlight were like brand new natural biological factors to Lindsay because she damned herself to the cabin with Smoke. She hadn't been outside of her cabin since she kidnapped Darnell. She refused to leave her precious Darnell for one second because she knew how quickly things could change. Lindsay had her guards do everything for her that she wanted or needed. She spent days and months trying to get Smoke to break from his Passive hex, but he just wouldn't do it. No matter what Lindsay did to him, Smoke was strong-willed.

Seeing Marcela was refreshing, because Lindsay hadn't had any contact with anyone either except for Darnell. It wasn't like he talked to her anyway. He refused to talk to her, touch her, look at her, acknowledge her, or any type of response gesture to her. Of course this angered Lindsay so she tried to hurt him countless times, but there was nothing more painful to him then being without Passive. Passive was the driving force that allowed him to still be alive without eating or sleeping in months. Call it brain power.

"Hey Marcela how you been sissy?"

"I've been okay please sit down and have a glass of this Pinot Grigio with me so I can talk to you."

"Please tell me what's wrong? I'm hating the blank expression on your face right now. This is supposed to be a nice lunch."

"There's really no way to say this so I'm just going to come out and say it. Two people in our family have been murdered. Our mother has been murdered and our cousin Novara has been murdered as well. On top of that British has taken over the house telling me about some will bullshit, but I'm not buying that. I really can't see our mother leaving everything she owned to British?"

"Your kidding me right?"

"I'm more serious than a heart attack Lindsay. I called you as soon as I found out." Marcela was staring at

Lindsay's face, and she saw a tear drop from her eye followed by another tear from another eye. Then Lindsay just covered up her face with the table napkin for a few moments until she could pull herself together.

"Maybe if I would've never kidnapped Darnell none of this would've happened. When I heard about mother being released from the center, I should've been there to take care of her, but I've been too busy torturing Darnell; torturing a man who has a wife and only longs for his wife. What the fuck is wrong with me? What kind of person am I? Please tell me you've been to Detroit to find out exactly how all of this happened?"

"I've been to Detroit, but ain't nobody telling me nothing, this is definitely your strong suit. If anybody can solve something I know you can. Don't beat yourself up Lindsay he knows you are mentally ill. You need to do right by this situation. Let him go back to his wife and hope that one day he will forgive you for everything you've done to him and his family. You've been out of business for too long this is not even you. Stop letting Nestle run your business before you never get it back."

"Your right Marcela you are so right."

"Have you been taking your medicine?"

"No I haven't this is my first time even being out my cabin since I kidnapped him."

"Well have you thought about getting help again so bad stuff like this won't happen anymore?"

"No I haven't and I really don't have time to think about it now. All I want to do is get back to Detroit so I can settle everything with mom. I'll be damned if I let that bitch British do anything else without my permission. She is not about to get rich off of my mother. I don't give a fuck what the will say. I will find that will and burn it to pieces."

"Okay Lindsay let's get something eat now." Marcela and Lindsay ended up getting some old-fashioned, crispy fish and chips and chatting it up for a few hours.

Marcela didn't feel any regret for helping Passive and them free Smoke at all, even though Lindsay was acting like she regretted kidnapping Smoke, Marcela knew her sister didn't regret anything. No matter how fucked up the things were that she did in her lifetime the word regret didn't exist in her vocabulary. Eventually, the two left each other, and planned to reunite again in Detroit to solve Liz's murder.

Chapter 14

The Triumph

When I am weak, I am still strong.....

Once the anti shady bunch got Smoke out of that hellhole he was being caged in, they all loaded up in the Caddy and Posh led the way. Smoke knew that he was going to escape from Lindsay, he just didn't know how or when, but thank god he had a determined wife like Passive. His rescue was a prime example of why he chose to marry her, why he did mischievous things for her, and why he killed for her. Passive Boone Mitchell was one hell of a woman and she had back-up. Smoke never thought he would see the day when Passive was bonding with other women because Passive was a mean girl. The only person she let herself bond successfully with was Smoke.

"These are my lovely ladies Smoke who helped me rescue you. I see you dozing off so I'll tell you all about them later," Passive wanted to properly introduce Elvia and Posh, but now was not the time.

Fortunately, Posh and Corbin had some property in New York where Smoke and Passive were going to stay for a little while just until things died down. It was going to be a long minute before Lindsay figured out who Passive was teaming up with anyway if she ever figured out. Despite all of that, Passive had an inside man now who ran by the name of Marcela and since Marcela didn't let them down, Passive had to disburse her some gratitude. Marcela was another woman in Passive's life who proved to have some dignity.

Passive's text to Marcela:

thank you Marcela we got him

Marcela's response

give him some well-needed TLC

Passive's text to Marcela:

see you soon

Abruptly, Posh brought Corbin up to speed with everything via telephone on the way to the low-key property. Corbin was chill with everything, and was pleased that Passive got her husband back, and the ladies accomplished their mission. Smoke hadn't had any real shuteye in months, so he was using this car shuttle as a sleep booster.

Nobody wanted to wake Smoke from his slumber, but Passive and Smoke had to get settled in. They needed to be alone ASAP, with no distractions, and no company. Posh gave Passive a quick tour of the house and dipped. Posh, Corbin, and Elvia were going to keep their guards up and stay checking in on their newfound friends, but now it was time for some outer space. Just like Smoke, all Passive wanted to do was sleep next to her king because nothing had been the same since Smoke had been gone anyway especially not the way she slept. The couple ended up showering and falling asleep together naked in the nearest bedroom. When Passive awakened it was all smiles. Smoke was delicately fingering Passive's hair and staring in her alluring green eyes.

"Smoke when you get ready you should call your mother and let her know yourself that you are okay." Smoke checked his ears to make sure his hearing wasn't faded.

"Baby you and my moms' is on good terms now?"

"I know everything about you and your mom Smoke. How you were writing her and been communicating with her all these years. All this time I thought you hated her, but I guess I never took the time to really get to know her. I apologize to you if I made you feel like you should shelter the part of you that needed a healthy relationship with their only parent."

"Who is this woman that you have become?"

"I'm a little mix breed of the Passive you first met in your police sanctuary and the Diamond we've created over the years with all of our shady embarks."

"Well damn what else did I miss?"

"Let's see where should I begin? I won your bike back from Gab and set his ass up in the hospital with a broken femur. I ended up meeting Elvia at the motorcycle races, but come to find out she had been trying to be on our team for the long scope. I met one of your ex-girlfriends Solei, who was going around town spreading stories about having you in her custody trying to obtain your reward money so I had to kill that bitch and her roommate. Did you know that bitch was a hermaphrodite and don't lie to me?"

"I didn't know until the bitch took off her clothes. I left that bitch in that same unfilled token so keep going."

"My hate with Lindsay was so deep that me and Elvia ended up killing her mother and her maid. Your ex co-worker Shania rose from the dead and tried to kill me, but Elvia killed her first. Your cousin and his motorcycle gang retaliated on our house by trashing it and trying to wipe us off the radius. Marcela ended up finding her way into the precinct so I coerced her and made her help me find you. And now here you are in my arms like you never left or was stolen away. By the way what are we going to do about that hideous tattoo of yours?"

"I'm getting this shit covered up as soon as we hit the MO when I find a good cover up artist. I knew that my queen could handle her throne. Don't ask me about how life was without you because I don't want to relive none of those empty moments I had to spend with that wench. I just want to continue to wrap myself up in your love."

"I know it may sound like it was an easy thing to do, but being without you was a pill that was hard for me to swallow. As you see I tried to put my Marvin daisies behind me, but I'm back to killing. "

"We knew this day was going to come sooner or later. Sometimes you can't run from life you have to embrace it and killing is an evolution of you. The way our lifestyle is we have to kill people. That's just the way it is."

"I love you Darnell "Smoke" Mitchell."

"And I love you Passive Boone Mitchell."

$

When Lindsay got back to her palace, she saw bullet shell casings everywhere, and her property was now unguarded because her guards were all dead guarding the ground. Off rip she knew that her precious Darnell was gone; she didn't even have to flee to the attic and look. She went from 0 to 100 real quick. She knew Passive must've got her flimsy paws back on him through somebody's grace. It was pretty foolish for her to think that Passive was just going to sit back and let another woman steal her husband from her anyway. Besides, love and goodness always triumphs over all. It was time to re-evaluate, regroup, and rethink because Lindsay's strategies weren't working on the dynamic duo. Lindsay came to the conclusion that she was putting way too much emphasis on Passive and Darnell as a couple and as individuals that she needed to go back to thinking outside the box. Something similar to the way she was thinking when she met Omani, and got Omani to kiss Passive.

The best way to get to somebody is by hurting people they love especially people who Lindsay would be least expected to hurt. Once upon a time, Lindsay did have a hit out on Omani and her boyfriend Onyx, but since her hittas weren't good enough to carry out a hit, the hit was uplifted, but the hate was still there. Lindsay just had to dig a little deeper than a garden shovel into Smoke's and Passive's lives so she could put her plan in motion.

Reverting back to Marcela's bad news on top of everything that was going on, Lindsay had to go back to the D so she could bury her mother, and deal with her conniving ass cousin British. Even though Lindsay's cousin Novara should've been a part of her burial arrangements, she decided that Novara's mother should handle her daughter's funeral not Lindsay. Lindsay wasn't the family funeral planner; she was just a person who happened to have the same last name as a bunch of other people whose last name was Chambers. The death of Novara Chambers wasn't her loss or her problem.

Thinking on her mother's murder not natural death, all types of thoughts passed through Lindsay's mind. Did Passive kill her to get back at Lindsay for kidnapping her and Smoke? Did British kill her so she could speed up her inheritance and get off the street? Or was her mother's murder just going to be another episode on 20/20 ABC? Whatever the fact of the matter was it was time for her to kiss New York goodbye and go back to the D. Before departing Lindsay stopped herself in her front door and gazed around. She was grateful for the time she had with Smoke, even though she had to kidnap him just to get time with him, it was what it was.

Chapter 15

Antennas

You don't have to lie to kick it....

One thing expectant mothers did best was waddling and shopping. Tia had just left a doctor's appointment and snuck off to meet her home girl Mila. Her and Mila had lots to catch up on and Tia had a chief question she needed to ask Mila. Onyx was going to kick her pregnant ass when he found out, but since Tia wasn't going to snitch on herself, she wasn't going to let him find out. What could a couple of hours really hurt anyway?

Auburn Hills, MI was the destination so Tia could hit up Great Lakes Crossing where some unwanted crossings where about to take place.

Omani was with her friend Giva when they bumped back to back into each other at the Motherhood Maternity Store.

"I'm sorry for bumping you," the two faces collided in remembrance.

"Omani is that you?" Tia asked with her eyebrows.

"Tia it's not a pleasure to see you here," Omani put her hand over her hip insinuating her enlarged baby bump.

"You should be ashamed of yourself walking around with a pillow in your shirt just so you can look pregnant."

Omani lifted up her shirt inside the maternity store and flashed her protruding stomach. Tia's jaw dropped instantly.

"This baby is realer then real. Would you like to feel my baby kick?"

"Onyx told me you got an abortion."

"I'm sorry please run that by me again," Omani widened her eyes.

"I said Onyx told me you got an abortion."

"That nigga ain't never fixed his mouth to say shit about no abortion."

"You must've really pretended really good then that you aborted the baby because you drove him right into my hands. Your pussy must not be shit because he put a ring on it."

"Fuck you blabbing about now?" Tia stuck her ring finger out, but remembered that Onyx still hadn't given it back to her so the jeweler must've still had it. All talk and no pull.

"Good luck to you and your keep a nigga baby." Tia tried to exit the store, but Omani stopped her.

"Not so fast, were about to have a lunch date with Onyx."

"Ouch your hurting my arm! Let it go! My antennas are up to, I'm not going to lie, but Onyx cannot know that I was here today. I'm supposed to be in the bed anyway."

"Whatever is going on with you, your pregnancy, and Onyx is not my problem, but the fact that he's been playing the both of us is. So I need your number and your address now. Call me when you get home and I'm coming over there to settle this fair and square tonight. All you

185

need to do is call me when he gets there and you better not forewarn him."

"I won't forewarn him because I want to know what's going on too so I'll see you later." Tia exchanged all the necessary information that she needed to exchange with Omani and took off.

"Oh my goodness Mila this is horrifying."

"Girlllll…. Who you telling like your baby daddy is going to get busted tonight. I wish this was going to be on pay per view because I want to watch, listen, record, and rewind this."

"Shut up Mila, but first I want to know if you'll be my baby's godmother?"

"Yes! Yes! Finally I'll be a fairy godmother!"

"Oh that's not all. I haven't told nobody this yet, but I'm about to tell you so don't judge me, but Onyx is really not my baby father. I just wanted to cause friction in his relationship with Omani so I told him I was pregnant by him. Everything else just happened on its own and I've been milking every single minute of it."

"You shady little bitch so who are you pregnant by?"

"Whom else? It ain't nobody other then my ex-boyfriend Rue. That's right he finally knocked a bitch up. I wanted to be sure about this and when my doctor told me my conception date I was sure whose it was and who's it wasn't." How sloppy of Tia to be messing with another woman's man. Guess she figured he hit it first with her so British's little premature vagina didn't matter. She was the queen of side bitching and now she got a baby out of it.

"You must love playing with fire."

"I do it's really befitting of me." Mila and Tia wrapped up their little mall date so Tia could get back home and pretend like she never went anywhere in the first place. Plus, she was dying to catch Onyx up in his 99 lies.

$

187

Around 8 o'clock Onyx came strolling through the front door baring gifts.

"Hey love," Onyx kissed Tia softly.

"I brought you a couple goodies since you've been in the house and haven't been able to go out."

"How thoughtful," Tia answered like Onyx knew Tia went to the mall today and was trying to make her feel guilty and tell on yourself. Since Onyx was here it was time to send Omani on her way so Tia shot Omani all the info she needed via text.

Tia didn't even care what Onyx had brought her so she just grabbed the bags he was holding out for her and took them to her room.

"Your really not going to look and see what I got you?"

"I'm going to look later if that's okay with you."

"You must be having them mood swings again?"

"I guess you can say that."

As Onyx and Tia were talking the doorbell rang and Tia broke wind to answer the door before Onyx did.

"Please come in." When Omani walked in the house Onyx couldn't believe his eyes. He didn't know what in the hell was going on. When did his two baby mommas become friends? Omani came with all of the things that Onyx had left at her house because she was tired of housing his shit. Omani didn't want to have shit to do with a man who would choose his side bitch over his main bitch and been going around lying just to kick it.

"So you been lying to Tia all this time and telling her that we decided to get an abortion together?"

"I did that and so what? Are we putting people on blast today because if we are let's talk about how you were laying up in the bed with me every single day and night daydreaming about your sister-in-law."

"So I share my inner most feelings and my secrets with you and now your trying to blackmail me?"

"I'm telling it like it is. I saw that magazine with you and her kissing. How in the fuck did y'all two dumb bitches come across each other anyway?"

"Dumb who you calling dumb?" Both Tia and Omani said at the same pregnant time looking at each other puzzled. Clearly, Onyx was caught off guard so now he was mad, but he did this to himself. He didn't have the right to be mad.

"I'm calling y'all dumb for ending up pregnant by the same nigga and taking the whole pregnancy just to figure out that I've been playing y'all both."

"So what your saying is you've been misleading the both of us intentionally?"

"Yep you hit it right on the nose. Omani I really thought you were going to get an abortion because I know the way you are and you can't be the way you are with a baby. A baby would only hinder you. And Tia I don't believe the baby your carrying is mine, I know you've still been fucking with Rue. Did you actually think I was going to wife a bitch who use to fuck and still fucks my best friend? I only proposed to you to play with your head just like you've been playing with mine. I just been here because Omani was on the verge of getting me killed."

Well damn! If that wasn't throwing shade then I don't know what is. "I'm out of here, y'all can keep my things, y'all can burn them, donate them, anything. And y'all can stay friends, y'all can even become best friends, but I could give zero fucks what y'all do. Omani I know that's my baby so just call me when you go into labor, but don't call me until then. Tia please lose my number and forget my very existence. I advise you to leave Rue alone before British finds out because once she does find out that you've been fucking her man she's coming for your ass. She is that type of bitch; she worse than Omani let Omani tell you how she is. And just like that Onyx was out.

Tia was just verbally destroyed, but she deserved it because Onyx wasn't miscuing Tia of anything. He was speaking the truth and only the truth. And now Onyx had Omani looking at Tia sideways.

"I'm highly confused and I don't know what's really going on here, but that ain't my baby inside your stomach so that issue doesn't pertain to me. And Onyx and I are over so I can't help you with that neither. And neither one of us is in the position to be stressed out right now so I'm just going to leave, "and just like that Omani was gone too without any hassle even though Tia wanted to explain herself. She was probably just going to add to the bullshit and keep the acting shit up, but the cameras were off now. Why do bitches always want to act? Why can't bitches ever be real?

Chapter 16

Snake Eyes

The inside of my eyes look like snake pits....

When Paradise was stressed out her remedy was a royal cup of tea. The Purple Door Tearoom seemed to be a new hot pub highly recommended for their tea so Paradise went there. It seemed like Paradise's Detroit family was all dodging a bullet because she didn't find haven with none of them. The life of a partial convict was the life she chose so all Paradise could do was keep it moving. Living out a hotel was getting old, but if celebrities could do it Paradise figured she could do it too.

If only Paradise could've stayed in Missouri and made her crooked relationship work with Cahill, she wouldn't be facing these Detroit dilemmas she was facing.

Sipping on her cold, sweet, addictive tea, Paradise got lost in her phone looking at some old pictures of her and Cahill. Next thing she knew she got the shock of her life.

"Since this seat isn't taken, I know you won't mind me sitting here, "Cahill surprised his boo thang.

"Cahill please don't be mad at me I had to leave without you knowing." Paradise was stuck. Chill bumps began to rise and fall like a slope to Paradise's skin.

"I am a mayor so I can fix any problem you have and you can always be found so don't ever think I can't find you. How has sleeping at the Hawthorn Suites been? They don't look as lavish as the kind of hotel I would put you up in. Tell me the real reason why you fled from Missouri?" In that same inclination, Cahill proceeded to take a knife out of his pocket, and stick it under the table in the middle of Paradise's vagina.

Pressured to answer accurately and concisely, Paradise damn near swallowed her tongue. "It's a lot of things you don't know about me and that's what has me shaken up. That's why I left Missouri."

"Things like what?" Cahill compressed his knife closer to Paradise's thin black fabric.

"I feel like Champagne's murder was all my fault. I participated in a heist, I ran off with some fraudulent money which means I left her there to die. I don't know who killed her, but I'm afraid whoever it is gunning for me next."

"I need names, why are you still acting like you can't communicate with me effectively like I'm not your man or something?" This time Cahill's knife cut through Paradise's leggings and now she had a little opening in them full of air.

"Champagne was dealing with some chick by the name of Lindsay Chambers who wanted her to kidnap Passive. Passive was one of me and Champagne's drug connects so we did a lot of drug business with her. So I'm afraid Lindsay killed Champagne, I really don't know whatever happened with the girl Passive."

Instantaneously, Cahill froze when he heard the name Passive, but he only knew of one woman named

Passive and that was his alleged goddaughter. Passive wasn't a common name so Paradise had to be referring to the same Passive he loved and use to cherish.

"What color eyes did she have?"

"She had green eyes. Why does her eye color matter?"

"I know this girl. She is supposed to be my goddaughter, but we haven't seen each other in years. Her father was my best friend until he got murdered. I highly doubt my goddaughter is dead she comes from thoroughbredness. I hate to hear that you and your friend kidnapped my goddaughter so y'all could rob her and who knows what else. At the same time I'm going to look past it because there are a lot of things that you don't know about me also. Who am I too pass judgment?"

Cahill left a brand new, bank printed 100 dollar bill on the table and yanked up Paradise before she even finished her tea. Clearly, there wasn't going to be no escaping this relationship, and she was now introduced to a side of him she had never seen before. Most men who give luxurious promises and are full of money bags usually have a dark side. In this case, Cahill had a shady side and now she was emending on this woman named Passive who she helped kidnap, who could be gunning for her too. Her mayor man was going to protect her, but how far would he go to protect her?

For one he had GPS navigation on his coochi and for two he just tried to cut her walls out just to open up their blurred lines of communication. Passive's money wasn't going to last forever though so Paradise mine as well just live it up with Cahill.

All of suddenly, Cahill's government Lincoln stopped. In response Cahill got out of the car to open Paradise's door for her.

"Baby, I got some investigating to do so you go upstairs and I'll be back when I'm finished. By the way this is your new guard Rock who will be watching over you 24/7 now. He will show you the way to our room. You just let him know whenever you want something and he'll make sure you get it."

"I don't want a guard Cahill all I need is you."

"I can't watch over you 24/7 plus it's kind of dangerous being my girlfriend, and this topic is not open for discussion so give me a kiss and I'll see you later." Cahill's and Paradise's lips touched passionately and she left him.

Cahill didn't have any business to do in Detroit because his new tower and power was only official in Missouri. It was some people who resided in Detroit that he had to do some long, lost visits with. He found his woman, brought her back, and put her ass on lock, check, and now he had to clean up her dirty work with some investigations of his own.

$

The bitch was officially back and just as British was exiting her and Rue's new playhouse, Lindsay was coming up the walkway. British looked up to catch a glimpse of a much unexpected, dreadful face.

"Oh Lindsay I didn't know you was coming into town I must be going though." British tried to pull a fast one, but Lindsay poked out her left foot and tripped British.

"When we're you going to tell me that my mother was murdered?" Still British was trying to find shelter with the ground. She didn't know whether to stay down or get up.

"And by all means you can take as many seconds as you need to think about it." British knew that Lindsay could and would end her life right here and right now on the cold, solid concrete if she didn't come correct.

"In all honesty I don't have your number and I didn't know how to get in touch with you. Then your sister Marcela showed up over here, and she promised me she would tell you everything herself."

"You probably lying, but that's what we Chambers were born to do." British dusted herself off feeling like she needed to go inside the house to change, but fuck her outfit. She just wanted to get the hell away from Lindsay's berserk ass now.

"All I want you to do before we finish this conversation is briefly tell me exactly how you found my mother."

"The door was open when I got here, but I didn't think anything of it until I walked into Corset's dead body, and then went upstairs and saw Liz's head cut off and cut open. There were S marks everywhere on her, and there was this word Smoke graffiti covering all the walls. I sanitized, repainted, and re-carpeted the house up so you wouldn't be able to tell none of that. And knowing the type of business you do I know you don't want to make any contact with the police."

"Well thank you for that little story because you have confirmed everything that I already knew. Marcela was telling me about some sort of will. It seems that my mother had a soft spot for you and she left you practically everything she owned."

"Yes that is true."

"So dig this, if you and your nigga want to keep everything she's giving you, I need you to do me a favor. I don't know what the favor is, but I need you to do it. I don't want your man to do it or nobody else you may know to do it. It has to be done by you. Otherwise I will find that will, burn it to smidgens, I'll burn your ass alive too, and keep your man for myself. I mean let's be for real you know how I get down. I don't make threats I make promises." British didn't know what the hell Lindsay was going to manipulate British into doing, but her hands were tied with this one. How could she refuse anything from Lindsay? Nobody crossed her, and if you did cross her you weren't going to get away with crossing her. Besides, it wasn't like British was a miss goody two shoes anyway. The only reason why she pretended like she gave a damn about her grandmother was to reap the benefits of her grandmother since nobody else gave a damn.

"I got you Lindsay, you know where to find me. You can always count on me to come through for you." Maybe British wasn't as bad as Lindsay thought she was. Finally she had a down ass family member who could come in handy.

Back to the murder scene and pondering on the clues, Lindsay knew it had to be Passive who had slain her mother. Lindsay never thought Passive would take things to that level or that Passive even had enough balls to put her hands on a trigger or even handle a weapon, but she thought wrong. Like Lindsay said back in New York, she had to start thinking indirectly and not directly because none of her other strategies seemed to have worked so she was about to do some dirt digging around the D to see what she could come up on. And since her phone was ringing, it wouldn't be long before she got hipped to something.

"I need to meet you somewhere now while I'm in town," a familiar male spoke which brought a vindictive smirk to Lindsay's face."

"Lucky for you I just got back in town myself so text me everything and I'll be there shortly." Things were about to get real shady.

Text to Lindsay:

Meet me on the River Walk by the Princess dock as soon as possible

Lindsay's response text:

I'm in route

When Lindsay approached the big, oversized
Detroit Princess boat her company was already there not
looking a day over 40 as usual. And he could sense her
steadily approaching him.

"It's been a very long time since we've talked."

"Yeah who would've thought that after Syrian's
death we would find ourselves doing business again?"

"Right, so first things first I'm sure you know my
old lady Paradise she use to run with the bitch you killed
Champagne."

"I've killed a lot of people, but I didn't kill
Champagne. You can pin that one on Passive."

"Okay so your not trying to ice Paradise are you?"

"I don't give a damn about no fucking Paradise! I
won't be the one to harm your girl. I got a million and one
more important things on my plate right now."

"What about Passive that's still my god daughter? I told you were never to kill her no matter what your deal with Smoke was."

"That bitch is a nuisance and I kept my word. I didn't kill her; I just set her up to be kidnapped."

"She could've been killed."

"Nobody would've missed her."

"Do I need to throw your ass in the Detroit River?"

"I'm good, my bad for that. Don't worry I won't be bothering Passive anymore. I'm done with bothering her and Smoke. It's other methods to my madness and I'm going to follow through with those."

"Whatever you do just don't undermine Passive because she's capable of more then what you think."

"Are you responsible for turning her into this monster or something since you know it all?"

"No her daddy is, life is, and you are," Cahill claimed like he wasn't a part of the problem too.

"I have some funeral arrangements to tend too, and I'll let you deal with Passive, but you got 90 days to deal with her. After 90 days she's all mine and I'm not sharing because that green-eyed bitch killed my mother."

"It was your idea to kill her father so aren't y'all even now? A parent for a parent; bloodshed for bloodshed right?"

"Once again I got somebody to kill him. She went into my mother's house and killed my mother herself. It doesn't matter; were done here. I'll catch you on the flip side." Cahill took off with the Canadian Bridge in his peripherals, and Lindsay took off headed towards the eastside of Detroit. Her business was done for the day.

Chapter 17

Naturally Painful

New life is a joy and a curse at the same damn time…

Fierce, intense sensations were hitting Tia below the belt like heavyweight jabs. Her body was painfully going through some type of transition and she wasn't ready for this birthing process called labor. Tia's first mind told her to call her bitch ass baby daddy, but Rue's phone was going straight to voicemail so Tia called back to back to back, but all she heard was that annoying ass automatic voicemail prompt programmed for every cell phone.

"Really Rue why fucking now? I bet if I was about to offer you some pussy you would answer. This is the time when I need your ass the most. Now your ass is dislocated because of your own faults. This is some real pregnant bullshit, but I'm not the first and I'm not goin be the last woman to have to endure this shit alone."

Every since Omani and Tia had confronted Onyx, Tia hadn't seen or heard shit from Rue. Even though, Tia and Onyx were in a relationship crisis, now was not the time for petty shenanigans.

Tia's next bright idea was too run her some bathwater and see if the hot water tranquilized her pain. She thought maybe she was imagining the pain because she was paranoid and annoyed at the same damn time. Too much was happening, things weren't right, Tia was so unprepared. She didn't have the car-seat in the car, she didn't have the baby's diaper bag ready, she didn't have her overnight bag ready, nothing was ready. Then it dawned on her, that maybe she was having contractions and maybe the baby was coming. Tia was so unsure, she felt so unprepared, she just wanted to go back to sleep, and she wanted the baby to stay in her womb a little bit longer.

Once the tub got full of hot, relaxing water, Tia hopped in and leaned her head back against the backside of the bathtub like she was chilling in a Jacuzzi. She had a few dry minutes without any pain, then like a stab there was that sharp pain again vibrating through her whole body. The contractions were getting harder, closer, and stronger which meant Tia had to do something quick, but she didn't have enough strength to make it out the tub. Every time she tried to get up and get out the tab, the contractions pierced her ass still causing her to freeze and clinch.

Tia had to call somebody now to help her, so finally she grabbed her phone, and just randomly selected somebody out of her call log. The person she magically selected was Omani which was even worst then Tia calling Onyx, but the phone was ringing, and this baby was coming so it wasn't no hanging up.

"Hello?" Omani answered wondering what the hell Tia could be calling her about since the two of them already confronted Onyx and wrote him out of their lives.

"Omani please help me I'm in labor!"

"I'm not a doctor what am I supposed to do?"

"Have you spoken to Onyx since we've confronted him?"

"I haven't had any communication with him and I don't want to have any communication with him. Fuck Onyx! And why are you concerned about him? You've been smashing the homie this whole time."

"You are in no place to judge me Omani. Can you please just call me an ambulance and send it to my house?"

"Just because we almost had the same baby daddy doesn't make us friends I still don't fuck with you the long way."

"Omani please I don't have anybody else to help me and I can barely talk. I really didn't mean to call you, I just dialed somebody and it happened to be you."

"Alright just this one time, but don't call me and ask me for no more favors."

Omani did exactly as she said she was going to do and she called 911 and got an ambulance sent over to Tia's house. Hopefully everything would go good with her delivery and for once in her life Omani could be thankful for not being shady. Even though, Omani was always on some shady shit, Omani was going to be having her little bundle of joy soon and who knows when and where her labor was going to break. She might need somebody to do for her the same thing she just did for Tia. Either way it went, Omani was changing for the better. Motherhood was actually becoming a good look for Omani.

Tia ended up giving birth to a healthy son she named Rhys Owen Powell in her living room with the help of two well-trained paramedics. After the two paramedics delivered her baby they got Tia and the baby up and out of her apartment and into their ambulance. To the hospital they went. An hour after Tia's arrival to the hospital and being placed in a room came a visitor. It was something about hospital visitors; those unsystematic motherfuckers were never good.

"I advise you to keep playing your shady little Onyx card because I won't let Rue have shit to do with your baby. I don't give a damn if he fathered the little bastard or not." British was in that thing trying to give Tia a new revelation about her parental life.

"British you have to be the dumbest bitch alive if you think I'm going to keep my son away from his father because his bitch said so. What I say always goes so don't think for once you coming up in this hospital throwing threats is going to make a difference."

"Why do you think I let Rue impregnate you? That shit didn't happen by accident. Bitch you was an open surrogate."

"I didn't have this baby for you so stop trying to play mind games with the livelihood of my son."

"You know Onyx's baby mother right Omani? Yeah I'm sure you do. Ask her about the Chambers and how we get down. The last thing you should want on your head right now is a Chamber. I wouldn't want your son to be brought up in this world without a mother or father. But actually all we have to do is get rid of you and then I'll be his mother. Hmmm... I never thought of that."

"Leave before I page security."

"Page security by the time I snatch out your IV and choke you with your own IV fluids you would be dead." Lucky Rhys wasn't in the room because things were about to get real ugly.

"I just came here to let you know that I know about you and Rue. I know I can be a little startling, but you should see me when I'm not bluffing." British blew Tia a kiss and left the room.

$

The Swanson funeral home had been withholding Liz's body for weeks and finally a family member reached out to them. As gloomy as death was, it was their duty to peacefully rest loved ones. Viewing Liz's body was not at all an option for Lindsay nor was having a funeral or a closed casket viewing where fellow Chambers' could say goodbye. Lindsay didn't associate herself with the Chambers' and the Chambers' didn't associate their selves with Lindsay.

Cremating Liz was the most practical solution to her mourning problems, so Lindsay made the proper provisions, and now it was time to get the ashes. Liz's ashes would never ever be forgotten or misplaced. Now that Lindsay had possession of her mother's ashes she could entomb her mother's ashes in her private, single, outdoor, mausoleum crypt. Marcela was supposed to be in attendance, but at the tempo that Lindsay was going, she didn't want anybody to accompany her. And she damn sure didn't want anybody to see her cry because Lindsay rarely ever cried, but a parent is something that can never be replaced. Losing a child has to be a relatable solitude as losing a sibling or a parent.

Even after Lindsay dumped her mother's ashes, she still couldn't believe she was gone. A whole lot of facts were ruffling her all at once; the fact that she never got to say goodbye, the fact that she was murdered, and the fact that Passive killed her. That was three facts too many.

"I promise you momma if it's the last thing I do. I'm going to get Passive back for killing you and this time she want see me coming. I know she did this to you and whoever helped her is going to suffer alongside her." Lindsay spoke spiritually to her mother.

$

While Lindsay was at the River Walk talking to Cahill, she saw a recognizable face out the corners of her eyes darting past her. It almost slipped her mind that she saw Omani sluggishly walking with one of her friends. Therefore, Lindsay steered her head quick beyond detection so Omani wouldn't know that her enemy was back in the D. Studying Omani, Lindsay couldn't miss Omani's big belly that was so big it was pointless for her to zip up a jacket. So the Mitchell family had a baby on their way? If

Omani's baby were to magically disappear then the Mitchell family would be in complete turmoil. Lindsay could tell by Omani's slowness and fat ankles that she was due any day now, and was clearly trying to induce her labor. Lindsay already had a favor on the floor and now she could talk to British so she could deliver her side of the deal. She didn't give a damn if British had to call every hospital in the Motown 24 hours a day. It wasn't more than 10 hospitals in Downtown Detroit that British needed to choose from so her job was not going to be that hard especially not if she wanted to keep her inheritances. Just like British ride or died for her nigga, it was time for her to ride or die for her cousin- the one that nobody fucked with. No matter what she was going to find Omani Mitchell and she was going to get Lindsay that baby if that was the last thing she did.

"This is going to be so epic," Lindsay whispered to herself.

Chapter 18

The New Mitchell Air

6 weeks after Smoke's return

Reunited like a family reunion, the majority of the intermediate Mitchell family was gathered at a buffet joint. The gang included Smoke, Passive, Kyra, Omani, Andrea, Zana, Posh, Corbin. Officer Rodgers, Rellow, and some of Smoke's other associates from the 11th precinct. Everyone was happy to welcome Smoke back home and repair their busted relationships. It was a welcome home party/baby shower where both Smoke and Omani got all the love. Plates were getting loaded and reloaded with the widest selection of food that the Golden Corral had featured on its layout. Omani was in heaven as big brother Smoke made sure she was peachy the whole time. He made all of her plates, refilled her refreshments, and made sure her appetite was completely satiated. He had so much lost time to make up for and he was really getting a good start.

Even though, Passive and Omani weren't on the best of pages before and during Smoke's kidnapping Smoke nipped their bullshit right in the butt. Omani was basically apologizing like 50 times a day to Passive

anyway, Passive was the one holding the grudge.

Days, weeks, months, and years weren't going to

pass by without this family being concrete. It was time that

this family matured, became supportive of one another, and

openly communicated with each other.

Smoke looked like the finest man in America again.

Life couldn't be happier. Both Passive and Smoke agreed

to wait until after Omani's baby was born before they killed

Lindsay.

"So either I just pissed on myself or my water just

broke."

"Omani you would know if you had to go to the

bathroom. That means the baby is on its way."

The Mitchell family wrapped everything up as fast

as they could, called Omani's doctor, and they got the q to

rush her to the hospital. All of Omani's family was here so

it was definitely perfect timing. Labor is a very

unpredictable stage of pregnancy, but now the wait was about to be over because contractions were doing sharp hammer times all inside of Omani's birth canal. Omani was taking her contractions like a pro because her face didn't drop any type of uncomfortable expression, she wasn't complaining, or crying. She was focused, she was calm, and she had her breathing exercises down-packed.

"All I ask is that somebody take my phone and call Onyx for me. We're not on good terms so I don't care if he comes or doesn't come, but he told me to call him when I'm in labor and since I'm in active labor, let's give him his call." Smoke snatched up Omani's phone so he could call her baby daddy and if Onyx knew what was good for him he would answer the phone because he didn't want Smoke on his head.

"Hello," Onyx answered like he had been screening Omani's call.

"Yea this Smoke and Omani is in labor about to have the baby. I better see your ass down here soon."

"I hear you Smoke. I told her I would be there for that. I give you my word on that." Onyx and Smoke ended their short conversation.

Unlike most women, Omani didn't know what the baby gender of her baby was going to be, but she was going to find out whenever she pushed him/her into the world.

Only two other people besides Omani were allowed to be in the room with her so she picked Andrea and Passive. Now after today, once Passive observed the whole laboring and delivering process, she wasn't going to be having any of Smoke's babies anytime soon. When Smoke found out Omani wanted Passive to hold a leg, he had to be an asshole like he always was. It just wouldn't be right if he wasn't an asshole.

"You know I married you so you could give me some green-eyed babies? Plus myths say if you interact with a pregnant person while their in labor your going to end up pregnant next. ”

"Shut up Smoke, you know we're going to have kids when we have them. I told you I don't want to plan anything. I just want to let it happen on its own. There's no rush because I'm never going to leave your silly ass. These pretty green eyes aren't going anywhere." Passive and Smoke were trying not to get too frisky in the visitor lobby, but when your madly in love with somebody you can't help but to throw yourself all over them.

"Are you nervous baby?"

"Damn right I am, I've never saw anyone have a baby before. What if she asks me if she can hold my hand and she squeezes my hand too death? What if she starts cussing me out just for telling her that everything is going to be okay? What if she gets an epidural and her epidural wears off?"

"Just be calm baby, my mother is going to be in the room with you. She is not going to let Omani scare you away. Besides my moms had three kids so she knows exactly what's going on all too well. Omani has a high tolerance for pain so I doubt these contractions are even grazing her."

"Well I'll see you when the baby gets here."

$

After 10 hours, 9 minutes, and 8 seconds, Omani Mitchell delivered a healthy 7 lb 8 oz baby girl vaginally at 39 weeks gestation. Omani named her baby girl Amory Daylyn Mitchell. Amory was the cutest little bundle of joy the Mitchell family had ever had. Andrea was now a proud grandmother, Smoke was a proud uncle, Passive and Kyra were proud aunts against all the odds Omani had. Now it was time for everybody to go home and let Omani bond with her baby girl alone.

Omani was content that the hospital she delivered at allowed her baby to sleep in the room with her. Since the baby was asleep, Omani went to sleep too. That was probably the best motherly advice that Omani would've ever received. "When the baby is sleeping, you go to sleep too or else you will never get any sleep." Somebody should've been watching over Omani though.

When Omani was sleeping a strange woman crept into her hospital room, slid Omani's baby into a book bag like her baby was a stuffed animal, hit the stairwell, and headed for the parking lot which was connected to the hospital. One thing this hospital lacked was infant security so there weren't any security tags or baby bracelets to set off any metal detectors.

Finally, Onyx made it down to the hospital to see his baby girl. He missed the actual birth, but some effort was better than no effort. As he was entering Omani's room, the first thing he noticed was an empty bed and a sleeping Omani.

"Omani, wake up," Onyx lightly shook the arm that was IV free.

"Onyx your late. I didn't even know that Smoke got a hold of you. I really thought you weren't coming."

"Where is my baby?"

"She should be in her bed asleep."

"There's a bed right there, but she's not in their sleep."

"So let's call a nurse then. They probably took her to the nursery or something. I'm sure it's nothing major." Omani pressed the nurse button on her hospital bed.

"Can I get you something?" The nurse on duty asked Omani courteously.

"Yes I'm trying to find my daughter Amory. She was in her bed sleeping when I went to sleep, but now she's not."

"Is this the father if you don't mind me asking?"

"Yes it is."

"You're a lucky man because your daughter is absolutely stunning."

"Thank you," Onyx responded proudly even though he had been a shitty person to Omani lately. None of that mattered right now. The only thing that mattered was Amory. That was the link between them two, and that was the only thing that mattered right now.

"Let me go check with the nursery and see if they took her for testing or something. I'll be right back okay."

"What the fuck is taking her so long Omani?"

"This is a hospital Onyx, me and Amory aren't the only ones here." Thirty minutes had probably passed since the nurse returned. Omani was starting to get real antsy now too. Finally, the nurse veered her face again and she came with backup because she had a feeling things were about to get real in Room 203.

"I don't know how to say this, but your daughter was not taken for any testing, she is not in the nursery, and none of the other staff have seen her or taken her."

"Where the hell is my daughter then? I trusted y'all, I delivered my baby here! Out of all the fucking hospitals in Michigan I picked this sorry ass hospital to have my baby thinking we were going to be in good hands. Ain't nobody in good hands here if y'all got newborn babies popping up missing!"

"Omani you rest I got this."

"I'm not resting. I can't sleep without our baby. She is the only thing right I got in this world."

"Y'all mediocre, non-care providing, inattentive motherfuckers better find my daughter now or I'm going to blow this motherfucker up!" Onyx started flipping over empty gurneys and deserted wheelchairs in a deep ire as he headed for the hospital exit ready to inflict, immense pain on the entire hospital faculty.

Chapter 19

D-Town Avenger

How shady can you get?

The groundwork of Smoke's and Passive's subsistence was ruptured and punctured like a fetal water bag. It was time for them to reconstruct their MO (Modus Operandi) because they had too many opposing forces. Too many people knew where the morning light cracked open their eyes and the night nestled them. All of their properties in-state and out-of-state properties had to be sold. All of their vehicles and motorcycles had to be sold and traded in too. Everything that was old had to go.

Passive and Smoke were going to build a new empire that began with them, Posh, Corbin, and Elvia. Running cities and capitals wasn't shit because the five of them were going to run countries and continents.

The new and improved residential city of the Mitchells' was Beverly Hills Village, Michigan. Their new house was shitting on their old house because it was an incredibly larger colonial, brick masterpiece. It had an indoor pool with a waterfall spa, sauna and full bath home.

It had a 3-car side entry garage and circle driveway. It had a finished basement with bedroom and bath. It had a 2/3 acre wooded lot for privacy and seclusion. There were a total of 5 bedrooms and 4 bathrooms with a total of 5,680 square feet; the list of amenities goes on.

Smoke couldn't wait to get back to work at the 11th precinct because he found out he was getting a new position, he had new fellow officers, he was getting a new office, and he was going to find a new scheme for him and Passive. Since him and Passive were settled in, it was time for him to get a new morning routine and a new work route going. First thing Smoke did when he got to the 11th precinct was stop at his old desk. When he stopped at his old desk it was a white envelope waiting for him on the surface and there was a hospital blanket folded up next to it.

Grabbing a seat, Smoke opened the letter and silently read it amongst himself.

Dear Smoke,

I thought we made a first-class couple, but in your eyes I guess we didn't. It seems when I kidnapped you that your wife went haywire and killed my mother. Of course I cannot and I will not let her get away with that. So I took my pretty little notepad out and I found somebody who might buy you guys a lot of more undisturbed, quality time together. Without me trying to kill you guys that is. Who would've known Omani was pregnant about to have a baby girl? Amory is her name right? Yeah that priceless little thing is with me. Omani wasn't supposed to even live to see the day when she could become a mother because I tried having her killed. Why want you Mitchells' just die? I don't understand why y'all consist of fighting me? Y'all are like electrical fireplaces; sometimes y'all are on, sometimes y'all are off, but once plugged back into a circuit y'all fire is right back burning again.

Well it's been real; I'm on baby duty now. Y'all

may have found me in New York, but I have tons of

real estate properties just like you and Passive do.

Ta Ta! Good luck finding me and Amory and

breaking the news to Omani. Now let's see what

sibling is going to hate who worst now?

Lindsay

Oh my God, this cannot be happening not another Lindsay travesty again. The last thing Smoke wanted to do was fret Omani, but he had to validate this information so he called Passive.

"Baby just answer me in yes and no answers real quick okay."

"Okay."

"Have you heard anything about Amory being kidnapped?"

"No."

"Have you spoken or been to visit Omani today?"

"No."

"Okay that's all I need to know. Great, now I have to call Omani so let me call you right back."

Hesitantly, Smoke dialed his sister Omani.

"Smoke I have to talk to you," Omani declared sniffling sounding like she was crying the Detroit River.

"Please just tell me you and the baby are okay?"

"Amory is missing, please tell me what to do, my heart is so broken right now?"

"I'm sorry to say this, but Lindsay wrote me a letter confirming that she kidnapped Amory. I found the letter sitting on my old desk today and I read it like 20 times already to make sure this is our life right now."

"Why would she do this? I thought that y'all had beef and me and her beef was tarnished since she kidnapped you? Amory is innocent. This is not chess; she doesn't deserve to be treated like some type of pawn. She needs me right now. She needs her father right now. How in the fuck am I supposed to tell her father that our daughter has been kidnapped by the same woman who tried to kill me and him both? He left me for almost getting him killed and now our daughter has to suffer because y'all keep letting this bitch live? Did you make some type of plea deal where she would free you and in your place would go my child? I mean you are a cop and that's what cops do? They do dirty shit to protect themselves and kill others because nobody sees cops as the bad guys."

"I know your hurting Omani, but I didn't have anything to do with this. That batshit bitch is obsessed with this family period and since she couldn't kill me or Passive she went for the next best thing."

"You was talking all that family shit at the restaurant, but fuck this family! I hate this family! I'm going to stay away from y'all and I want y'all to stay away from me like y'all have done so many times when I fucked up. Y'all the ones that fucked up now though and got my baby kidnapped! Now I got to file a missing person's report and put an amber alert out for my baby who is not even a day old! Don't try to contact me unless y'all find my baby. Believe it or not, I'll go 100,000 miles in a hospital gown until I find mines and bring her back home." Click.

There was a new set of drama all over again.

Now it was time to call Passive back.

"Are you going to tell me what all the yes and no's were about now?"

"Lindsay kidnapped Amory and Omani is going ham on me." In that instance, Passive's heart was in shambles.

Damn that bitch works quick; that bitch must've found out I killed her mommy. How was the funeral bitch? I bet you the funeral home was more empty then a can of pop after the last sip.

This is a grown-up game why she wanna involve a little

infant? I targeted adults, but I guess anybody can get it

now. I can't even imagine how Omani must be feeling, but

maybe next time she will consider having a home birth

because you can never be too careful. Whether you have

enemies or not shit like this happens in the world every day.

I thought I was going to be able to get Passive together a

little bit and work on some of my own aspirations, but I

guess Diamond never gets any rest. So I better go get the

girls together so we can find my niece and finally

annihilate the beast (Lindsay). I told myself anyway after

Omani dropped that baby Lindsay had to be dealt with. The

shady gets shadier, and if this is the shadiest she's got, then

she better go watch Lifetime or Snapped and take some

pointers. Muah vacation and separation it's been real, and

I got to hit the road again.

"I guess we're going to be on another shady mission again babe."

"Yep you know I'm always down for another mission."

THE SHADINESS IS NOT OVER

IT'S TO BE CONTINUED….

www.ingramcontent.com/pod-product-compliance
Lightning Source LLC
Chambersburg PA
CBHW071855220626
47052CB00002B/135